THE *Sister* WIFE

A TEST OF LOYALTY DUET - BOOK ONE

DAPHNE KANE

CONTENTS

Copyright © 2023 by Daphne Kane

All rights reserved.

No part of this book may be reproduced in any form or by any electronic or mechanical means, including information storage and retrieval systems, without written permission from the author, except for the use of brief quotations in a book review.

This book is a work of fiction. Names, characters, places, and incidents either are products of the author's imagination or are used fictitiously. Any resemblance to actual events or locales or persons, living or dead is entirely coincidental.

Cover by Mayhem Cover Creations

Get new release updates and exclusive content when you sign up for my mailing list.

To my sister.

The holder of my heart. Thank you for always lending me one of your breaths, when I didn't have one of my own to breathe.

I love you, chick.

AUTHOR'S NOTE

Please be aware that the content in this story might include graphic references to mental health topics, such as panic attacks, PTSD, depression, and mentions of suicide. If you or someone you know is having thoughts of suicide, the National Suicide Prevention Lifeline is available twenty-four hours a day at 988.

CHAPTER ONE

January 25, 2018

Naomi

Nathan, you no good motherfucker!" I screamed as the vase I hurled across the room exploded above my husband's cheating head, causing shards of glass to rain like confetti on him and the bitch he was fucking in our bed. "That's okay. I got something for you and that bitch." I spun on my heels and rushed out.

"No!" I heard him shout once he realized where I was going.

"Please stop screaming, and you might want to get out of here before she comes back," I heard him say in a rushed tone.

"But Nathan, Mr. Warren said—"

"Look, just get your shit and go!" he yelled.

The soon-to-be-dead bitch didn't pick up that her life was in grave danger, but Nathan had.

"This is how that no good motherfucker wanted to play with me." I swung the closet glass door open with so much force, it bounced off the wall and shattered.

"I've got what your dirty ass needs right here," I screamed through hiccups as I swiped away snot and tears that ran down my face. On my tippy-toes, I stretched to grab the gun case from the highest shelf. Breathing heavily, the hurt and pain tried to consume me, but they were no match for the angry beast raging inside and wanting out.

"I've given up everything for you. I moved across the country, away from my friends and family. I've been an amazing wife to you, a good mother to your child, and this; this is how you repay me? Not today, Nathan. Not to-mother-fucking-day, you bastard!"

I turned around, stumbling over my evening gown as I rushed to place the case on the counter. I swiftly punched in the security code, but before I could open it, I was pushed up against the counter, the wind forced from my lungs.

"Let me go, Nathan. Let me go right now, got damn it!" I screamed and struggled against his large frame.

"I swear if I were facing you right now, I would rip your dick off!"

"Baby, please, just hear me out." He grunted as he struggled to restrain me.

"Baby, please, my ass. You're only making this worse; let me go, Nathan."

"It's not what you think. Please hear me out."

"Not what I think? You can't be serious right now; you are literally standing here with your dick out!" I would have laughed if I wasn't out for blood.

"Baby liste—"

"Let. Me. Go. Nathan!"

His body tensed. I took advantage of his stunned state and began to struggle earnestly. He was losing his grip. With all gentleness gone, he clamped down like a vise, trapping my arms, and spots danced behind my eyes.

"Stop this, and listen to me," he whispered harshly into my ear.

We stood like that, breathing roughly.

"Baby, I need you to listen to me. I know I fucked up, okay. But please, please let me explain." When I hadn't interrupted, he continued.

"I made a mistake, okay. I fucked up Naomi. I fucked up badly. Why would I do some dumb shit like this to you? To us? You and Livy are my world, baby. You're the best thing that's ever happened to me. Please calm down, and let's talk about this. We can fix this baby, okay. Just trust me." He paused again to gauge my reaction.

"I can't lose you, Naomi; I can't. We can work this out." My shoulders began to shake. "Come on, baby, please don't cry." He tried to turn my face toward him.

I lifted my head, leaning it back on his shoulder as I laughed. I laughed at how heartbroken I was. I was such a fool.

"Let me go, Nathan."

"Naomi, look—"

"Let me go so I can lock the gun back up."

He relaxed a little. He didn't release me completely, but enough to do what I said. After securing the case, he spun me around and hugged me tight.

"Thank you, baby, thank you so much. You are the best thing that's ever happened to me." His words were heavy with relief.

"You're right, I am. Now you'll have to live with the fact you just lost me."

12:20 a.m.

I sat at the light, clutching my chest, as the pain from my broken heart ripped through me. My tears continued to fall as I shook my head in disbelief. I'd been driving aimlessly around Austin, Texas, for hours now; my tired mind needed rest. I may not get much sleep, but I needed to find someplace to at least rest my eyes. My scratchy eyes could make out the bright yellow-and-black Best Buy sign ahead. I entered the large vacant parking lot and pulled into the first stall. After I cut off the engine, I released a heavy, defeated sigh. *Now what am I going to do? Who am I going to call?* I have no one here in Texas but him. A bitter laugh left my lips at the only person that popped into my head. After a few moments of going back and forth, I finally said *fuck it* and made the call. After the third ring, I heard a groggy "Hello?"

Here goes nothing.

"Tess, it's Naomi. I … I need you."

CHAPTER TWO

Naomi

"Naomi? … what's wrong?" Tess asked on alert.

I took a couple of deep breaths before I told her what happened.

"Ah, man, I'm so sorry, Naomi."

"What happened, baby?" I heard a deep voice ask through the phone.

It was Teddy, Tess's husband.

"It's Naomi."

"Is everything alright? Does she need help?" His caring tone caused my heart to clench.

"She's fine. She's coming over and going to sleep in the guest bedroom."

"Okay, let me make sure it has everything she needs to make herself at home."

"Thank you, baby."

As I listened to their sweet exchange, my eyes filled with tears.

"It's going to be okay, Naomi," Tess reassured, hearing me

sniffle. "You come on over and let Teddy and me take care of you. Don't worry about Livy; she's in the room sleeping with Nya. Are you okay to drive, or do you want me to come and pick you up?"

"No," I croaked, "Tess, are you sure this is alright? I don't want to impose; I will understand if this is too awkward—"

"Stop, Naomi; I'm about to turn the porch light on for you and make us some tea if Teddy hasn't beat me to it. I don't understand how a man his size can be so domesticated and hospitable." She laughed, making me chuckle despite my pain.

"Okay, I'm on my way."

"Great, see you soon, and please drive safely. Bye, girl. *That no good bastard,*" I heard her say while hanging up the phone.

I exhaled a weary sigh as I put the Houston, Texas, address to my husband's ex-wife's home into my GPS.

"How could he do this to me? In our home, Tess? In our bed? What if our daughter was home? Wait, do you think he's done this before? How many women? Oh, god!" I cried out.

"Oh Naomi, I'm so sorry." Sorrow shone in her warm brown eyes. "I swear, I'm going to kick his ass the next time I see him," she said through clenched teeth.

"How are you doin', Little mama?" I heard Teddy's deep voice ask from the doorway.

"I'm okay; thanks for asking, Teddy."

"Good, the guest bed and bath are all set for you; if you need anything, please don't hesitate to ask, okay? And I just checked on Livy. She's cuddled up and sleeping in her big sister's bed."

I did my best to give him a smile of gratitude.

"All right, if you need anything, just text; I'll be upstairs."

"Thank you, baby; I will be up once I get Naomi settled."

When he was gone, she looked back at me. "I know you're

hurting right now and mad as hell, as you should be, but I don't think it's a good idea for you to make any rash decisions. Not tonight."

"Says the queen of rash decisions," Teddy mumbled from the staircase.

"Hush Teddy," she shot over her shoulder before calmly continuing. "All I'm saying is that you don't have to make any decisions right now. You and Livy are welcome to stay with us as long as needed. You don't have to worry about anything, okay."

"Thank you, Tess. This must be weird for you. Your ex-husband's wife is calling you in the middle of the night for help. How pathetic I must look right now," I said with a bitter laugh. *Damn it, Nathan. I hate you for putting me in this position.*

"Stop, Naomi. We're not enemies, nor is it written anywhere we're supposed to be. We've known each other for over six years now. I know we're not close, but I'm happy you reached out to me. I'm sure not too many women in your position would have put their pride aside and reached out. So listen, for however long you need to be, you and Livy will be here with us. I know that Nate Jr. and Nya will love having their baby sister with them. So no more worrying; let's get you settled." She finished, pushing up from the table.

As she led me from the kitchen through her gorgeous home, my mind replayed everything that transpired tonight. I had to be in shock as my mind processed that I was now a guest in my husband's ex-wife's home.

Something caused me to stir in my sleep. I wasn't ready to wake up, so I rolled over and tried to find the comfort I had moments ago. I froze when my hand landed on a warm, hard chest. *I must be dreaming;* I went to bed alone. My body relaxed as I drifted into a dream—a damn good one, going by the muscled flesh underneath my hand. As I settled into the dream, my hand slowly perused the smooth muscled flesh. I rolled in close, raising my left leg to cover my dreamscape man with the amazing body. After releasing a sigh, I melted into comfortable bliss. There was no pain of betrayal or sadness here. A smile tugged at my lips as I ran my hand further down the smooth chest. I leisurely continued to rub before trailing over perfectly sculpted abs. *My god, it was all so glorious,* I ruminated, running my hand lower to see what other treasures awaited. A zing of excitement ran through my body when my fingers ran across the top of a waistband. I brought my hand back just enough to slip my fingers underneath the elastic to continue my exploration of my dream Adonis. As my fingertips grazed the top of his pubic hair, I froze when the hard chest began to rumble with laughter.

"You might want to stop right there. If that hand goes any further, I promise, love, I will have to take over from there."

My eyes flashed open, realizing this was not a dream. There was, in fact, a strange man in bed with me! I did two things at once: screamed bloody murder as my fingers closed around his heavy semi-erection and squeezed it for dear life.

He hollered like a wounded animal as he tried frantically to escape my grasp.

"What's going on here?" I heard from behind me as the door opened and the lights blinked on.

"Oh no," I heard Tess say as she laughed.

"Tess, stop laughing and get her off me, damn it!"

He continued to scream as my mind tried to decipher if I was still in danger and needed to rip his dick from his body. The damn thing felt like I was holding a log. *What the hell?*

Still laughing, Tess calmly said, "Um, Naomi, can you let him go, please? It's only my brother, Rob. I'm sorry he disturbed you.

When he comes into town, he usually sleeps in this room. I promise he didn't know you were asleep in here."

I breathed deeply, trying to slow my pounding heart.

"I'm sorry if I frightened you, but now that you see I'm no threat, could you kindly release my dick," he gritted out.

I instantly released my hold before murmuring an apology.

He was no longer in my grasp and immediately rolled off the bed and stood. He leaned forward, resting his hands on his knees, closed his eyes, and breathed.

I took in his discomfort as my eyes went from his hunched-over frame to a laughing Tess.

"I'm so sorry, Naomi. I know that had to have scared the shit out of you; come on, you can sleep with me. Teddy can go to the den.

As I scooted to get out the bed, Rob said, "Really, Tess, you're going to ask if she's alright when she just tried to detach my dick from my body!" He grunted as his heated stare landed on me.

"Why are you looking at me like that? Once you realized the bed was occupied, you didn't think to find somewhere else to sleep?" I threw his way, as my embarrassment turned to annoyance.

"First off, when I entered this room, it was too dark to see anything. After working a long shift, I was too damn tired to do much more than take off my clothes and slide into *my* bed. I didn't expect anyone to be in it. I didn't realize you were there until I was under the covers. Imagine my surprise when a soft body rolled against me rubbing her hands all over me?"

"I didn't rub my hands all over you," I told him, feeling my cheeks heat up. "In my defense, I thought I was dreaming. What about you? You would just lay there and let some strange woman rub all on you without doing anything. What if I was—"

"Okay, you two, everyone is tired; let's get some rest. Come on, Naomi, let's go to bed," Tess said softly, leading me from the room.

I gave him a parting evil glance and I followed her out the door.

~

I slowly opened my heavy eyes, greeted with rays of warm sunlight softly bathing the room. I blinked a few times, turning my head to take in my strange surroundings.

Where in the hell am I?

Nathan.

Nathan, you son of a bitch, I groaned, closing my eyes again as a shuddered sigh left my lips. Everything that happened the past twenty-four hours began to replay like a tragic movie, from the fundraiser to catching him having sex with a woman in our bed. Now I knew why he backed out of attending the fundraiser with me at the last minute: I wouldn't be home until late.

I worked on that damn fundraiser for the past three months to ensure everything was perfect. It was going to be a big event that many well-known and important people were planning to attend. I knew this because he told me constantly. Being a good wife, I volunteered to help out. I was going to make sure my husband shined. I wanted to impress his boss as well as future clients. I was in charge of many details, from booking the servers and dancers to finding an ice sculptor to pull off what we were going for. I even donated one of my Kirkland Vaughn original paintings for the auction, which was expected to bring in a lot of money. I'd worked hard on this, so we had to be there, right?

We were all dressed up, ready to leave. I wore a black strapless satin evening gown with a sweetheart neckline and a high side split to complement his black Vera Wang slim-fit tuxedo.

We looked hot. Right when we were about to leave, he swayed a little on his feet.

"Baby, are you alright? I asked, looking over his beautiful face.

"Ahh, yeah, I just need to sit down for a moment," he said with a tremor in his voice.

I dropped my things on the stool and helped him to the couch.

"Baby, what is it?" I asked, scanning his entire body.

"Damn it! I haven't had one of these in a minute. Why tonight, of all nights, do I have to get the migraine of all migraines." He raised his hand to massage his temples, too upset to look at me.

"Oh baby, it's not your fault."

We were quiet before I said, "Listen, we have a couple of options here, and I'm down for either. I could run upstairs to grab you some pain medicine and see if that helps, or we could say to hell with it, go back upstairs, take these clothes off, and climb into bed."

"Baby, I can't ask you to do that. You have worked too hard on this fundraiser," he said with sadness reflecting in his lovely hazel eyes.

"And why not? You are my husband. Baby, your well-being means everything to me. I can call Cynthia and explain what's happened. I know the fundraiser will be in good hands."

When I turned to make the call, his arm shot out to stop me, taking me by surprise. I lifted my questioning eyes to him and waited.

"Baby, listen to me; you worked too damn hard on all this. Every free moment you had, you were doing something for the fundraiser. It would be a crime if you weren't there tonight."

"What are you saying, Nathan?" I asked him, absently shaking my head. He couldn't possibly be suggesting that I go without him.

"Baby, I'm sure all I need is a little rest; I should be better tomorrow—"

"No, Nathan; absolutely not! I'm not leaving my sick husband's side to go to some damn party."

He tried to chuckle, but it turned into a grimace. "That's why I love you, you're so good to me and Livy, but baby, I'm going to need you to be there tonight. Mr. Warren will be there with his wife. It's already going to look bad that I won't be there, but at least seeing you, he may be a bit more forgiving. Plus, after he sees what you pulled off, I'm sure he will want to sing your praises, and that will only make me look even better in the client's eyes."

I took in everything he said; I wanted to make him look good, but leaving him didn't sit right with me.

I guess he could see I was about to say no because he hit me with, "Baby, aren't we a team?"

"Yes, you know we are."

"I need you to do this for me, Naomi. When I'm weak, you have to be strong."

Those words made me cave.

I released a defeated sigh as a smile ghosted across his lips.

"Alright, Nathan, I will go."

"Thank you, baby," he said, removing his jacket and tie. "I'm going to bed, but I want you to try to have a good time. Do you hear me, Nay?"

"Yes, I hear you," I said reluctantly.

He gave me a weak smile before turning to trek back up the stairs.

~

The Fundraiser

As I glanced around the buzzing banquet hall, my chest swelled with pride. The gleaming black-and-white checkerboard floor pattern beautifully complemented the black-and-blush-pink decor throughout. Black shimmering sequined tablecloths were draped over every table, topped with tall crystal vases and lighted branches in the center. The pops of vibrant greenery cascading down represented wealth and prosperity. Everything looked fantastic. I wished Nathan were here to add to the ambiance. I slowly turned and walked toward the alluring black grand piano in the corner of the room. *Well done, Naomi, you have outdone yourself, girl,* I complimented myself as sadness settled in my chest, knowing Nathan wouldn't get to see it.

"Naomi, everything looks amazing!"

I turned to see Carole, Nathan's boss's wife approaching.

"Thank you, Carole," I said, smiling warmly.

"Are you sure you don't host private parties or gatherings? I have friends who would hire you in a heartbeat to turn their homes into this during the holidays. She finished with the sweep of her hand around the hall.

"You're too kind, thank you for the compliment, but no, I'm an artist. I could come out and paint a custom mural or some art to complement your lovely home. I've worked with different mediums like gold leaf and resin to create unique designs."

"Aw," was all she said with disappointment. "An artist, well, that suits you, dear. With that hair or lack thereof," she said with a chuckle. "Well, I will keep that in mind. If you'll excuse me, I see someone I would like to greet over there."

Whatever, I thought. *I've been a stay-at-home mom since moving to Texas six years ago; I'm dying to get back to work. Working on this fundraiser has proven that.* I peeked down at my watch for the hundredth time. I had been here for fifty-two excruciating minutes. I kept thinking, what if Nathan had an aneurysm and couldn't call for help?

That's it; I'm out. I can't be here when my husband is sick at home.

On my way home, I stopped by the store to pick up the things I needed to make homemade chicken soup and pain medicine for his headache. If he still wasn't feeling better by morning, we would go to the ER whether he liked it or not.

I pulled up in front of our house, and a car I had never seen before was parked in our driveway. I know, good and well, our neighbors didn't have one of their guests park in our driveway. Just because it was late and there was no car there, does not give them the green light to use our driveway without asking. How long have they been doing this? That's okay; I'm going to have Nathan go over and talk to Todd tomorrow; this is unacceptable. I marched up the steps and unlocked the front door before I tiptoed inside. A smile crested my lips, happy to be home early, ready to love on my husband for the rest of the night. The last thing I expected to hear walking inside my home was loud … moaning.

What in the entire fuck?

I quietly placed everything on the counter, slipped off my high heels, and made my way upstairs.

As I got closer, it became clear what was happening, but sometimes the mind plays tricks on you. I had to see this with my own eyes. My heart started to pound, and my ears began to ring.

I know this man isn't in there doing what I think he's doing. He can't be. Nathan isn't that crazy.

Nope, it's got to be a porno, but why would he be watching porno if he's so sick and that damn loud?

As the questions continued to assault my mind, and trying desperately to come up with any logical explanation for my soon-to-be-dead husband, I was barely aware of my hand reaching out to grab the heavy crystal vase off the landing as I walked by.

With my bedroom door straight ahead, my mind tried one last time to reason with me.

"Stop, Naomi, that's not Nathan's voice you're hearing; it can't be. He wouldn't do something like this to you. It has to be the man in the porno that just so happens to sound exactly like Nathan when he's having sex. Yeah, that's got to be it."

What the fuck ever, I kicked the door opened and aimed the vase at the back of his lying, cheating head.

Too bad I missed.

"Oh my god, Nathan, you've broken us?" I whispered as I brought my palms to my eyes, trying to hold back my tears. This wasn't a cruel nightmare. He cheated on me in our home. And now I was here.

As my new reality began to set in, I felt real panic when that familiar dark cloud in the recesses of my mind peaked out at the first sign of my distress.

Oh no. I thought as fear gripped my heart.

"Get it together, Naomi, get it together, get it together, get it together." I chanted over and over as I focused on my breathing. With my emotions scattered everywhere, it wasn't easy to get centered, but I had to try.

After a few moments, I could think about the situation rationally.

Yes, I'm devastated. My life was just blown up, but I couldn't fall completely apart for any reason.

You can get through this, Naomi; you've gotten through worse. I tried to replace hopeless thoughts with positive ones.

"Pull it together. You've got this. Think about Livy; she needs you," I said out loud with a shaky voice. "You're strong; this will only break you if you allow it. You have a gorgeous little girl that's happy and thriving. This is on him, not you. You've been a great wife. You're hurting right now, but it's not the end; you will survive this. What doesn't kill you only strengthens you, and I'm a living testament to that."

I continued to speak light and positively.

Once calm, I took a deep, cleansing breath and sat up to take everything in. The first thing I realized was that I was alone.

Good.

I crossed my legs, closed my eyes again, and tried to breathe purposefully. The last thing I wanted to do was meditate, but it was crucial more than ever right now. *Damn you, Nathan.*

I blocked out the questions that kept trying to bombard my mind. *How could he do this to me? What am I going to do now? Where am I going to go?*

I sat still, trying to refocus my mind as I continued my breathing exercises. Deep breath in. Hold. Release.

I was so focused; I barely heard the light knock on the door.

"Hello, are you decent?" a male voice called out.

I looked toward the door as Tess's brother poked his head in.

"Ah, I'm sorry. Were you resting?" he asked.

"Um, no, just meditating; how may I help you?" I asked, tilting my head to the side.

"Yeah, um, Tess wanted me to tell you to take your time; you can come down when you're ready. She is in the kitchen making breakfast."

"Thank you for letting me know."

When he didn't turn to leave, I asked, "Is there something else?"

"Yeah," he said, massaging the back of his neck. "I wanted to apologize for last night."

"That's not necessary," I told him, shaking my head. "I'm the one that should be apologizing. I was in your bed and, well, for … grabbing you." I gestured toward his, *I'm sure*, extremely sore penis. Instantly, I was hit with a pang of regret as discomfort covered his handsome face.

"Well, waking up to a strange man in bed with you is under-standable. You went into fight or flight," he offered with a smile. "Plus, it's not my bed. I'm in the final year of my residency at

Houston Methodist Medical Center, which is not too far from here. Sometimes I crash here after a long shift when I'm too tired to drive home. Tess and Teddy were kind enough to give me a key so that I could come and go as I pleased and not disturb anybody when I got in. I wasn't expecting anyone to be in the bed. Again, I'm sorry if I scared you."

Listening to his deep baritone voice soothed something inside me. I appreciated him coming in here to explain, but he had nothing to apologize for. I was the one in his space.

I shouldn't even be here in the first place.

Not wanting to think about the reason why I was there, I told him, "No worries; I'm sorry for overreacting the way that I did. I'm Naomi, by the way. I'm …"

What in the hell am I supposed to tell this man?

"I know who you are, Naomi," he said, giving me a beautiful smile. "I've met your gorgeous daughter a few times when I came over to hang out with my niece and nephew."

"Oh, okay," I replied, relieved I wouldn't have to explain who I was or why I was there. "Well, it's nice to meet you, Rob."

"Okay, and take your time coming down. Tess will be downstairs with the kids."

"Thank you," I called out as he closed the door.

Why are these people so damn nice? I moaned as I flopped back against the bed.

"Why, Nathan? How could you do this to me? Now what am I supposed to do?

CHAPTER THREE

Naomi

Get up, Naomi; you can't hide out in here forever, I thought as I slowly got to my feet. I needed to return Tess and Teddy's bedroom to them. When I stood, I was reminded I hadn't used the bathroom in hours. I had to pee, *bad.* I looked toward the double doors to the left, where I assumed to be the master bathroom. *Nope, too personal.* I'd go out into the hall and find the guest bathroom. With a plan, I finally ventured out of the room.

After I found the guest bathroom and used it, I went downstairs. I needed to see my baby.

I wasn't familiar with Tess's home and didn't feel comfortable roaming around, so I did the next best thing. "Hey, is anybody here?"

I glanced around the gorgeous home, taking in the warm earth tones and peaceful vibe.

"Girl, if you don't bring your crazy ass in this kitchen." I heard Tess's light laughter carry from down the hall.

I remembered where the kitchen was from last night, so I turned and headed in that direction.

"Hey Naomi, how did you sleep?" she asked.

"Good, thank you."

"The kids are in the den watching a movie. Come sit down so we can talk. Do you prefer coffee or tea?"

"Coffee's fine. Thank you."

"Naomi, please stop thanking me for every little thing. You'll have me looking over my shoulder to ensure my mama isn't here. Checking in to see if I'm being hospitable like she drilled into me," she said, giving me a smirk.

"Well, she did have to test. You are rude as hell to have a mama like Ms. Peggy Sue Mason," Rob offered, walking into the kitchen.

He sat in the chair beside mine before he turned to face me.

"I know I told you who I was upstairs, but let me properly introduce myself; I'm Robert Mason, Tess's handsome younger brother." He finished while offering me his hand.

"I'm Naomi Wells, but you already knew that, and about last night, again, sorry," I told him with a sympathetic smile, placing my hand in his.

"No more apologies; we're good. I'm sure I will regain feeling down there in a day or so."

He laughed at my mortified expression while looking down at my wrist.

"This is nice. Real nice," he said as he inspected my bracelet.

I swiftly removed my hand from his grasp thanking him.

We sat silently, drinking our coffee, listening to Tess talk to Teddy in the other room. I could smell his amazing cologne as I felt his eyes on me, but I did my best to ignore him and continued to sip my coffee.

"So, what are you two getting into today?" he finally asked.

"We're going to have a girls' day, maybe go to the salon for a mani-pedi. Why, do you want to tag along?" Tess said, walking back into the kitchen.

"Naw, not my thing, but you go on and have a good time. Well, I'm about to head out. Teddy and I are meeting Terrell at the gym. I hope you both have a wonderful day today." he said as he got to his feet.

Tess raised her cup, silently wishing him the same, as he turned to leave.

"Well, have a great workout," I called after him, not knowing what else to say.

"Why, thank you, I will." He delivered a slow devastating smile before he slipped out the door.

My eyes lingered on the closed door when I sensed eyes on me. I glanced over to see Tess leaning against the counter, drinking her coffee, watching.

"What?" I asked.

"Nothing, what do you want to get into today? I just told him that because it's none of his business. What're we getting into?" She looked at me, waiting for a reply.

"I'm not sure just yet," I shared warily. "Try to figure out my next move, I guess. Make some calls to set some things up." When I finished, my heart thumped in my chest.

"Okay, but I think we should get out of the house. We could do a little shopping, maybe take the kids out. Whatever you're up for, I'm here, okay? But I don't think it's a good idea for you to sit in the room reliving what that wretched ass man did. I know you're hurting and sad; if you need to talk, just let me know, okay?"

"Thanks, Tess."

"No problem; I will be in my office if you need me. It's the door to the right of the front door." She walked out, leaving me alone in the kitchen.

After checking on Livy, I went back up to the guest room, not wanting my baby to see me upset. I sat on the freshly made bed and grabbed my cell off the nightstand. I slumped forward, thumbing through all Nathan's urgent texts. They ranged from pleading with me to come home to demanding where and who I was with.

Feeling sadness, I placed the cell against my chest, laid back on the bed, and looked up at the spinning ceiling fan.

What was I going to do now? Our future once seemed so clear, but now I was living in a nightmare.

I hardly left the guest room after having coffee with Tess, feeling pathetic and broken to interact with people. That evening, I heard a tap at the door. I wiped my tears and slipped off the bed to answer it, and Tess was holding a plate of food and something to drink.

"Tess, you didn't have to bring me a plate; I was going to come down," I told her, wiping my face.

"Here you go," she said, handing me the food. "If you're feeling up to it, come on down; if not, don't worry about it. There's always tomorrow, and don't worry about Livy; she's fine."

"Tess, are you sure you're alright with me being here?"

"Listen, Naomi, I know this may feel odd for you, being here in my home, but please understand where I'm coming from. I promise it's not odd for me. I'm happy you did call because, let's be honest, how many women as distraught as you were last night would have called their husbands ex? Hell, they probably couldn't. I think you and I have always had a cordial relation-ship. We had to; that's why you were comfortable with Livy coming over to spend the night with her siblings, just like I was comfortable knowing my kids were safe and cared for with you and Nathan over the years. It just all worked. You already know my Livy is welcome here any time; I need you to know so is her mother, okay? So please try to relax; you're already dealing with a lot."

Looking into her beautiful eyes, identical to her brothers, I nodded and said, "Okay."

"Now that husband of yours," she said, shaking her head and wagging a finger. "His ass knows he's better off sleeping underneath a bridge before he ever calls me for help. And that's all Nathan's doing. Teddy and I tried being cool with him, but with Nathan always having something slick to say, over time, Teddy stopped trying. But that's on his sorry ass. Anyway, enjoy your food, and we will talk later." She turned and walked back downstairs.

Over the next few days, I did my best to engage with Tess and her family. They were all amazing. I tried to ignore the uncomfortable feeling that sat in the pit of my stomach; it was a lot of work to keep a smile on my face as I was dying inside. I missed my home, even though I despised the man in it. Despite how quiet I tried being, I had a feeling they heard me crying in the room. Hearing a knock on the door jolted me from my thoughts. I wiped my eyes before I said, "Come in." I expected to see one of the kids, Tess, or even Teddy, but I saw a stranger.

"Can I help you?" I asked, watching the handsome, heavily muscled stranger walk further into the room. "Uh, can I help you?" I repeated louder, in case he was hard of hearing.

"Relax, woman, ain't nobody trying to do anything to you," he finally said. "I'm Terrell, Teddy's brother and Rob's best friend."

Now that he mentioned it, I saw the resemblance. I grinned; he looked like a baby Teddy.

"Ah shit, you've made the connection, don't even say it." He rolled his eyes.

"Excuse me, what?"

"You see me as little Teddy, or worse, baby Teddy, like everyone has our whole life. Well, as you can see, I'm big too. Maybe not as big as him, but I am nothing to sneeze at." He winked.

"I'm Naomi."

"I know who you are; I wanted to run up here to meet you and to tell you a few things about me. First, I'm a straight shooter and extremely blunt. I don't mean to be rude; I take after my mother; she's the same way. With that said, Nathan is a whole bitch; I've been telling them all this for years. Hell, I've told him to his face. You may as well get used to my handsome face because you will see it often around here. By the way, you have the cutest little girl; she is funny as hell. I'm going to make sure you're not sitting up here sad, feeling weird about being in your husband's ex-wife's house because, let's face it, it's kinda weird, but weirder shit has happened, and I won't allow you to stay cooped up in this room pining away over that wack ass dude. So please don't fight me on this. I can already tell you and I are going to be besties. Now grab your shit, and come on, let's go and grab a bite to eat while I tell you how fabulous I am. And hurry up; I'm an impatient man," he said and was gone.

What in the hell was that? I laughed, got out of bed, and grabbed my shoes and purse before I went to get to know my new "bestie."

CHAPTER FOUR

TNT Fitness

Rob

"**D**amn, she's cute," I grunted as I bench-pressed.

"He's got good taste; I'll give his sorry ass that. I don't know what these women see in those light-skinned Shemar Moore type dudes. Can his soft ass defend you if something jumps off?" Terrell asked, standing in front of the mirror doing curls with fifty-pound dumbbells. "And that's some cold shit to be fucking some broad in your wife's bed, man. That's bold as hell. I mean, did he not check to see what time Ladybug was supposed to be home? You got to plan shit like that well in advance; ask me how I know," Terrell said with a side-eye.

"Wait, who in the hell is Ladybug?" I paused to look over at him with a frown.

"Naomi. She reminds me of a cute ladybug with that haircut," he said, doing his curls.

A ladybug? Yeah, I can see it.

"That's just not cool to do someone you love like that, Terrell," Teddy chimed in with annoyance.

"Look, I can't say a girl has never walked in on me getting with another chick, but I've never been married. On top of that, I would never do no shit like that in my wife's house."

"In your wife's house? Meaning it's cool to do it someplace else?" I asked, making sure I understood where he was coming from.

"Well, yeah, all I'm saying is that it's going to happen somewhere."

"So, you're basically admitting that you're going to cheat on your wife when you finally get married, right?" I stopped lifting and looked toward him, breathing hard.

"Of course," he said, moving away from the free weights and snatching up the jump rope from the floor. "When I do get married, I plan to treat my wife like the queen she is. I plan to love and cherish her, but there's no way one woman can fulfill all my needs. And I don't expect her to; that wouldn't be fair. I mean, my sex drive is bananas, man. I'm being courteous."

"And you don't see anything wrong with that?" I asked, trying not to laugh.

"Nope."

"What if your wife has a problem with that?"

"She won't," he said, jumping in place. "How can she have a problem with something she doesn't know about?"

"So you have it all figured out, huh?" I asked.

"Yep," was his simple reply.

"That's where you're wrong, baby brother," said Teddy, who'd been resting between reps listening in. "On some level, she will know, so again, I ask how can you do someone you're supposed to love like that? I have a simple solution for you, just don't get married. Play the field if that's what you want, but don't bring someone into no bullshit. I swear if I see that bastard, I will kick his ass."

That made me laugh because Teddy was a gentle giant. His sheer size would scare any man, but he'd always had a soft spot for my sister Tess and crying women.

"Well, you don't have to worry about me. I know for a fact; I'm never getting married. I have no desire to be tied down to only one woman. I tried that once, and look how that turned out?" I laughed without humor, not meeting their eyes.

"No, Brie was a straight bitch for what she did to you!" Terrell yelled, no longer jumping, causing people in the gym to glance our way.

"Terrell," Teddy warned.

"It's okay, Teddy, I'm good. Tee was only stating the obvious; it's cool."

After that heated exchange, we moved on and finished our workout.

On my way home from the gym, Naomi crossed my mind when I first got a good look at her. It was the morning I peeked into the room. She was sitting in bed meditating. I studied her briefly before her gorgeous eyes snapped to me. I remember thinking she looked like a beautiful mocha-colored genie with her pretty bald head and delicate features. I first noticed the silver Cartier love bracelets on her wrists. I knew what they were at first glance. Those suckers cost a pretty penny. I bought Brie one similar for her birthday one year.

I released a heavy sigh as I slid down in my seat. *What in the hell made me bring Brie up?* Just the thought of her put everyone in a foul mood. It'd been over a year and a half; I hated the fact that she still crossed my mind.

"Alright, enough of that," I turned the music up, looking forward to the rest of the day.

CHAPTER FIVE

Naomi

While making the bed, I paused to count the days. I'd been with Tess and her family for seven whole days. Nathan was probably worried sick not knowing where I'd been, but I could care less. I did send him a text that read, *We're fine, but I don't want to talk to you right now. I will text when I am ready.*

And the only reason I felt compelled to do that was because I didn't want him filing a missing persons report.

I shook my head as I completed my task; I couldn't think about him right now. I had to make sure I didn't lose my damn mind. After placing the beautiful lemon-yellow comforter on the bed, I grabbed the matching pillows from the chair and arranged them neatly on top. I swear, I was still questioning my sanity for reaching out to my husband's ex-wife for help in the first place. That goes to show the mental space I was in that night. Clearly, I wasn't thinking straight because who does that?

I grabbed my cell phone to text Tess; it was time for us to talk.

Hey Tess, can you come up to my room when you can?

After sending the text, I tidied up the space, grabbed the new black yoga pants and purple T-shirt I picked up from Target, and walked into the bathroom. I bought a few more items I needed and some things for Livy since we'd been away from home for so long.

I hurried into the bathroom to change.

~

Tess sat perched on the side of the bed and waited for me to begin.

"I want to start off by saying I cannot thank you enough for all you've done. Taking me in when you could have just as easily turned me away; with that said, I know it's time for me and Livy to go."

She nodded. "You and Livy are always welcome here, but may I ask, where are you planning to go?"

"Probably back to California."

She sat deep in thought. "If that's what you want to do, Naomi, but I hadn't heard you mention anything about going back to California; I figured that wasn't something you wanted to do."

She was so damn perceptive because she was right. Going back to California was something I wasn't sure I ever wanted to do. There was just so much disappointment there.

"Are you sure, Nay?"

I released a shuddering sigh. "Yeah, I think it's for the best for now." I wasn't completely honest at the moment, but it was time to leave here.

She exhaled a hard sigh. "Okay, just know, I've enjoyed having you and Livy here, and I'm going to hate to see you leave." A small frown creased her forehead.

"You weren't planning to leave before Nate Jr. and Nya's

upcoming birthday party, were you? I would like for Livy to be there."

"Of course, we're staying until then." I smiled to put her mind at ease.

"Good," she said, relieved. "I don't know how I'm going to break it to the kids that Livy is moving, but I will figure it out."

I hated the idea of splitting up the children. Livy loved her brother and sister so much. Watching them made me think of my siblings and not talking to them. My older brother Kenny and I had never been close, but my baby sister Zena and I were once close, and I missed her.

"Tess, please don't say anything to them just yet; let's wait until after the party, okay?"

She agreed with a knowing smile as she got to her feet and walked toward the door.

"Hey, I wanted to see if you could help me out this afternoon?" She turned back to ask.

"Sure, what do you need me to do?" I asked, listening intently.

"I have a two-thirty appointment this afternoon with a new client. Do you think you can keep the kids busy around that time?"

"Of course," I replied, glad she was asking for my help.

"Thanks, girl. I will be meeting with the sweetest little boy and his parents today. He has sensory issues, and I don't want to risk setting him off with Nate Jr.'s video game or the girls' loud squealing."

"I got it covered; as a matter of fact, I will take them for a walk around that time."

"They're going to love that." She finished with laughter in her voice because she knew, as I did, the girls were going to complain.

"Thanks, Nay."

I laughed as I waved her thanks away with a flick of my wrist as she walked out.

~

After talking to Tess, I hurried downstairs to make some lunch. I was impressed when I first found out Tess was a speech pathologist. Anything dealing with impairment or disabilities of any kind I was passionate about. I'd worked with children on the spectrum in the past and volunteered at Livy's school. Tess let me know that quite a few of her clients were nonverbal, so it was best to have sessions when the house was empty to work with the children and their parents. My respect for that woman went through the roof, hearing how passionate she was about helping bridge the communication gap between children and their families.

"Hey, Ladybug, where are you off to?" Terrell asked from behind.

"Hey, Tee." I turned around, happy to greet Teddy's baby brother. *What in the hell was their mama feeding them when they were little?*

I cannot get over the amazing shape these men were in. Rob was the smallest out of the three, if you could call a man six foot three with a muscular, athletic build small. Next was Terrell at six foot four, with hard muscles popping out everywhere. I liked to call him the bite-size Teddy to get under his skin. I told him it was my way of getting him back for calling me Ladybug. Lastly, there was Teddy. I used to be intimidated due to the sheer size of him. Because of his impressive size, he worked hard to put people at ease. Not only did he have a sweet nature, but he was also gorgeous as hell. All three of them were. It really should be a crime to be that good-looking. It really should.

"Tess has a new client coming over, so I'm taking the kiddos for a walk."

"Cool cool, you want some company?"

"Yes," I said, happy he would be tagging along. "The kids would love that."

All three of the kids loved Uncle Rob, but it was crazy Uncle Tee that got everybody excited.

"You're not working this afternoon?" I asked him.

"Naw, Teddy's got it. We're opening another gym in Houston; he's with our lawyers now, finalizing some contracts."

"That's great news! In an article the other day, I read that TNT Fitness was one of the best gyms to join in Houston; that's pretty amazing."

"Yeah, whatever, just make sure you get your butt to the gym so I can whip you into shape."

"I'm down; just let me know when. I was about to make lunch before I had to round up the kids, did you want to join me?"

"Did you say lunch?" he asked, rubbing his hands together and licking his full lips. "Looks like I got here just in time, Ladybug."

This man. I rolled my eyes, chuckling, and walked into the kitchen.

Yesterday was a lot of fun. Terrell's good-natured personality never failed to put me at ease, and the children adored him. I smiled as I stepped off the front porch and tucked my AirPods in my ears. I decided to go on my walk early today. I wanted to do something fun with the kids later. I closed my eyes as the light breeze kissed my face. We were still in the cooler months, which I preferred. Texas heat could be brutal. It was a good thing I cut all my hair off long ago; my thick hair wouldn't have stood a chance in this heat. California could get pretty hot, but I had to get used to the heat with high humidity down here, but I loved it.

A smile crested my lips as I passed Tess's elderly neighbor sitting on his porch drinking his morning coffee.

"Good morning, Naomi," he cheerfully said once he spotted me.

"Good morning Mr. Thomas; how are you this morning?"

"Fine dear, you be careful on your walk, I believe I saw a coyote the other morning, and we don't know if it's rabid. A childhood friend of mine lost his life to a rabid coyote when we were kids. I've never liked them suckers since. If you want, I could tag along to ensure no harm comes to you."

"Thank you, Mr. Thomas, but I got it. I will make sure to find a big stick, just in case."

"Attagirl!" he said with a hardy chuckle.

I waved my arm in the air as I continued on my way.

The neighborhood was gorgeous and always so peaceful. It had a small-town charm about it that I loved. As I picked up speed, my artistic eye recognized the obvious beauty—the large front yards and majestic oak trees lined the streets. Everything was so picturesque. *I'm going to miss this.*

Maybe my eyes were playing tricks on me, but the sky seemed to darken. My time here was almost up. If I moved back to California, things would be very different and not in a good way.

Someone honked their horn. I turned to see Rob pulling up beside me.

"Hey Naomi, I knew that was you. How are you on this fine day?" he asked, propping his arm on the window.

"Hey Rob, how's it going?" I asked, pulling my AirPods out, noticing his nice fade.

"I asked you first, beautiful."

"I'm great, thank you for asking, and you?" I chuckled.

"I'm good, I'm good; I was on my way to check in on Tess and the monsters."

"They're all at the house. I'm pretty sure they're all up by now," I told him, pointing down the street.

I turned back to him to catch him smiling at me.

"What?" I asked with a furrowed brow.

"Nothing, you are always so pleasant. Have you always been that way?"

"Um, yep, pretty much," I told him, toying with my bracelets. "I mean, don't get me wrong, I do have a bad side."

"Oh, don't I know it?" he said pointedly, making me laugh. "Listen, I was going to take Nate Jr. and Nya to get some ice cream a little later before my shift. Is it okay if Livy tags along?"

"Um, sure, that girl loves ice cream, so I know she'll love to go. Thanks, Rob."

"Hey, would you like to come with us? I don't know if you've had the chance to go by the Underground Creamery, but some say it's life changing. I don't know about all that, but why don't you come so that you can be the judge."

Real smooth, I thought with a smirk. "No, you guys go on and have a good time."

"Alright, but it's your loss."

"I'm sure it is, but don't worry, I plan to check it out soon. I am an ice cream connoisseur, so I will tell you if the title is warranted."

"Okay, we won't be gone too long, and make sure you keep the volume down on those AirPods; I know this is a nice area, but you can never be too careful. Also, Mr. Thomas told me he may have spotted a coyote the last time I was over."

"Will do," I said, trying not to laugh.

He gave me a wink before he drove off. I finally chuckled and waved after him. I didn't know why I got so nervous talking to Rob. With Terrell, he usually teased me or made me laugh so hard I hardly caught my breath. Whatever the case, they were both super cool men.

~

"Hey Naomi," Tess called out, walking into the kitchen.

"I meant to tell you, the twins' birthday party is next Saturday. I'm unsure if you've spoken to Nathan yet, but he will be there."

"I know. He's been calling every day, but I haven't wanted to talk to him. I know it's time for us to have a conversation, though."

"Okay, I wanted to give you a heads up and let you know once more that you and Livy are welcome to stay here for as long as you would like, so don't let him pressure you into anything, okay."

The kids burst through the door from the garage.

"Here, Mommy, it's sooo good; try it," my baby said, offering me some of her ice cream.

"Kids, please go wash your sticky hands and do not touch anything until you do. Livy, go with your brother and sister to wash your hands," Tess called over to her.

"Okay," she sang, running out to wash her hands. I licked her ice cream and closed my eyes.

"Mmm, this is so good!" I moaned, savoring its cool creamy goodness. It tasted like cotton candy with lucky charms. I knew my baby picked it because it was pink and girlie, as was the taste.

"See, I told you. You should have taken me up on my offer," Rob said, strolling in. "It's good, right?" He asked as he sat across from me."

"You didn't lie; it is good."

"The best," he whispered with a wink.

Tess chuckled as she stood and walked to the sink.

I continued to eat my baby's ice cream when Rob said, "So I've been meaning to ask you, why are you bald? What's with the short haircut?"

"Excuse me?"

"Ah damn, I'm sorry," he said, leaning back in his chair. "It isn't health related, is it?" he quickly asked, looking up to meet my eyes.

"Um, nope. I just like rocking a short cut."

He cleared his throat. "Well, let me just say, that cut looks good on you. Not too many women can pull that look off as good as you. You have an aesthetically pleasing shaped head."

Tess coughed to hide her chuckles from the sink.

"Um, thank you, Rob," I said, not sure what else to say.

"No, really, the slope from the back of your occipital bone down to your neck is gorgeous and elegant—"

"Okay, Rob, I get it; you like the hook on the back of my head," I told him, trying hard not to laugh.

"Lord, I know this man didn't just comment on her head," Tess laughed. "Smooth, Robert, real smooth, commenting on the woman's hook head. 'You have a cute-shaped head,' that's all you had to say, man."

After a moment, we all cracked up.

Rob

I stood in the shower allowing the hot spray to beat across my tight shoulders. After a few more blissful moments, I reached for the handle to shut it off. I'd been in here long enough, but I didn't make a move to get out right away. I remained standing there with my hands pressed into the shower wall. A low whistle left my lips as I hung my head, thinking about *her* again. I'd been trying hard not to notice, but it was becoming more difficult the longer she was around. She was fascinating to watch. I loved her with my sister or seeing the joy on her face when she was out back, playing or singing with the kids. Everyone knew my niece and nephew were my whole world; I loved to see how happy she made them. She always seemed to strive to be happy. It was refreshing to see and be around. I breathed as I finally stepped out, grabbed my towel, and walked into the room.

I grabbed my cell phone off the dresser to check the time. *Damn, I'm going to mess around and be late if I don't get out of here.* After putting on my clothes, I entered the closet to grab my shoes. My hands paused as my mind wandered to Naomi once more. Occasionally, when she assumed no one was watching, I caught sadness masking her pretty face as she played with her bracelets. More than once, I had to stop from going to her, demanding she tell me what was wrong so I could fix it and see her smile again.

A noise caused me to look up; Tess stood in the doorway. *Watching.*

"Hey, baby brother," she said in that all-knowing tone I hate.

"Hey, sis, how's it going?" I asked as I sat in the chair to put on my Nikes.

"I see you have a lot on your mind; you want to talk about it?"

Time to go.

"Nope," I told her, kissing her cheek and walking out the room.

I could have sworn I heard her laugh when I reached the front door.

Whatever, I thought, walking out the door.

Rob

I swear, I can't catch a break this week! My eyes feasted on Naomi through the sliding glass door to the backyard as she gracefully transitioned through another yoga position. I'd been gone for a whole week, and what was the first thing I saw walking through the house? Naomi. I damn near forgot my reason for coming over in the first place as I continued to watch her. She wasn't skinny by any means. She has some meat on her bones and strong, defined muscles in her arms and thighs, yet still soft and luscious. I couldn't take my eyes off her.

"You see something you like?" Teddy asked from behind as he walked into the kitchen to stand beside me.

"Just watching Naomi do her thing. I love how disciplined she is, you know," I told him with arms crossed, never taking my eyes off her.

"She is that; she would have been a beast in the military," he said with a chuckle.

"So, uh, listen, you don't think this is a little stalkerish, you standing here, watching her yoga routine?" He finished with something reminiscent of a smirk and a twinkle in his eyes.

My face heated up, feeling like I'd been caught. "I was actually about to go out there and ask if I could join in."

"You?"

"Yeah, I mean, why not?"

"Robert Mason?"

"Yes," I huffed out, my nostrils flared.

"So you were about to go out there and ask to join in on … yoga?"

"Look, what's your point, Teddy?"

"Nothing, only making sure," he said, lifting his massive hands in surrender.

"But I can distinctly remember you stating yoga was for women and hippies years ago."

"I know what I said," I snapped.

"Well, I'm happy you finally came around and are ready to

embrace the benefits. Yoga is a practice. It helps not only physically but mentally as well."

We stood there in silence as we continued to watch Naomi.

"Are you sure the real motive isn't you wanting to get close to our house guest? And before you think about lying, I'm going to tell you what I told Terrell. Naomi is a guest in my home; her space will be respected; you feel me?" he asked with all playfulness gone.

"First Tess, now you." I sighed. "Yeah, I got you, big man."

"Good, let's go out there and see if we can join in," he said with a devious smile, knowing damn well I had no real desire to do yoga.

"Whatever, let's go," I grumbled.

CHAPTER SIX

Saturday, February 17, 2018
Twins Ninth Birthday party

Nathan

I *don't know why Tess didn't have the party at Chuck E. Cheese, as I suggested.* I mused as I pulled up in front of my ex-wife's home. As soon as I stepped out of the car, I could hear loud music and the squeals of children's laughter. I walked around to grab the twins' birthday presents from the back seat before I closed and locked the door, following the music and bright colored balloons toward the backyard. After walking through the side entrance, I came to a dead halt.

What the hell is she doing here? The last person I expected to see in the backyard, sitting entirely too close to Tess's brother Rob, was … Naomi. My Naomi?!

"Oh, she's trippin'," I murmured under my breath. Aside from a single text, I hadn't heard from her in all this time, and now she wanted to make an appearance.

"Before you flip out and make an ass of yourself, I need you to know I invited her and Livy weeks ago. Don't your trifling ass start no shit, or I will have Rob and Teddy carry your slow ass out of here, you hear me?"

I couldn't help but cringe hearing my ex-wife's voice. I turned around to confront the bane of my existence: Tess.

With her arms folded over her large breasts. "She is the mother of *my* children's little sister; just because your sorry ass fucked up with her doesn't mean the children should suffer. Nate Jr. and Nya are crazy about Livy; there was no way their baby sister wouldn't be here today. And you also need to know Naomi is under my protection while she's here. If you get out of line or harass her in any way, I can promise you won't like the consequences," she said with an evil smile on those beautiful lips.

Tess was a gorgeous woman. She always had been. Standing at five foot six, her honey blonde pixie cut and ruby red lipstick against her warm caramel complexion was the icing to her beauty. To top it off, the evil woman had a body that wouldn't quit. Her in-your-face personality was the opposite of Naomi's sweet and quiet disposition. It just didn't make sense. *How long have they been all buddy-buddy?*

Tess challenged everything while we were married, from where we lived to what I spent money on; Naomi was the total opposite.

Absently, I looked over in her direction.

What in the hell is she even doing here? "So you're going to sic your big ass husband and brother on me?" I chuckled, turning back to confront Cruella de Vil in the flesh. "Wow, Tess, you're really out here trying to take my whole family away, my wife and all," I told her smugly, trying to get under her skin. But I forgot who I was talking to; I should've known better than anyone; there was no getting under that woman's impenetrable skin. I recalled with a clenched jaw.

I cringed when she laughed. The sound grated my nerves as I prepared for what was coming.

"You mean the wife that walked in on you fucking another woman in *her bed*. I didn't have to take anything from you negro; you ran them to me. Naomi was so distraught catching your limp dick ass; the only person she had to call for help was me. Your ex-wife. Imagine that. You know she has no family here in Texas. And listen …" she squinted her evil eyes and pointed a long fingernail directly at me "… while she and Livy are under my roof, you will not bother her, do you hear me? Give her some time to see what she wants to do; you're the one that fucked up. I'm hoping she leaves your sorry ass, but that's just me."

"So this is where she's been hiding all this time, huh?" I asked in total disbelief. "So what, my wife and ex-wife are besties now? What kind of 'The Sister Wife' type of shit y'all got going on under this roof, with my children here?" I was momentarily distracted when Naomi's angelic laugh reached my ears. All I saw was red once I turned to see Rob, which was the source of Naomi's laughter, as they continued to sit entirely too close for my liking. *What the fuck is this?* I felt my body tighten up as I turned to walk in that direction on autopilot.

"Remember what I told you, Nate. Your ass better behave."

Tess's words at my back caused me to momentarily pause as I marched over to confront Naomi. I closed my eyes and took a couple of deep breaths to reign in my anger before I reached the giggling duo.

"Daddy, you're here!" I saw Livy frantically waving at me from the jungle gym.

I smiled, waving back, happy to see my princess. That happiness was short-lived as I continued over to her mother.

"Naomi, can I speak with you for a moment?" Her body stiffened hearing my voice. She tried her best to compose herself. She wanted to protest, but knowing her and not wanting to make a scene, she stood and walked to the side to give us some privacy. With her arms crossed and a bored expression, she waited to hear what I had to say.

The first thing I noticed was how pretty she looked today. She was wearing a teal maxi dress with spaghetti straps and silver sandals. I saw her favorite bracelets on each wrist and silver hoop earrings that sparkled every time she moved.

Here goes nothing.

"Look, Naomi." I ran my hands down my face. "I said I was sorry; I don't know what else you could want from me. I know I fucked up, but it's time for you to come home. I miss my family."

When her expression didn't change after my heartfelt request, I said, "What, you think you're going to continue staying here in my ex-wife's house with her family?" I scoffed, instantly regretting those words when her eyes turned cold. Shaking her head in disgust, she turned and walked off.

Damn, I thought with a frustrated sigh. I walked over to place the presents on the gift table.

"I see you're over here fucking up already. Huh, Nate?"

I closed my eyes and counted to ten.

"And since you mentioned it, we did extend the offer for her and Livy to stay here with us for as long as they would like," Tess continued from behind.

I turned to see her smug face, sipping her drink. Her arms folded as she leaned against the door frame. When I was about to tell her to mind her fucking business, Teddy's big muscle-bound ass stepped behind her filling the entire door frame.

One day, I swear to god, one day. I vowed and stormed off to greet my babies.

Nathan

After the birthday party, I hung around after deciding to take the kids to spend the night with me. They probably needed to be reminded that I was their father, in case they were over here being told otherwise.

I tried to catch Naomi alone for the past thirty minutes. She was avoiding me. I couldn't help noticing how comfortable she was walking around Tess and Teddy's home, which thoroughly pissed me off. Every time I looked up, she was talking to either Teddy, Rob, or Terrell. *I have to get her away from these big-ass niggas.* I pledged, watching them over my cup.

I bet they're slow as hell with all that muscle weighing them down. I sneered. Out of the corner of my eye, I caught Naomi heading toward the bathroom; I put my cup on the counter and hurried over. *Here's my chance.*

I stood right outside the bathroom and waited for her to come out. *She can't avoid me now.*

As soon as the door opened, I said, "Hey Nay, hold on for a second; I wanted to talk to you before I headed out."

"Nate, I don't want to discuss this right now," she replied warily.

"I don't want to either, but listen—"

"Ladybug, you cool?"

Ladybug? Who in the hell is Ladybug? I peered down the hall to see Terrell's big ass staring at us, waiting for Naomi to answer.

What the fuck was going on over here? *They already got a nickname for her?* I tugged at my collar and felt my temperature rise. Let me get it together. If I made a scene, it would only defeat my purpose. I waited for Naomi to answer him, even though it killed me. Once she nodded to him, he continued to where everyone was at. I turned back to her.

"Look, I understand, but we'll have to talk sooner than later. I was also going to ask if you needed a ride someplace?"

When she continued to stare, I lowered my voice and whispered harshly, "Come on, Naomi, I know you're not planning on staying here; I mean … it's weird and disrespectful, don't you think?" I smirked, trying to make her see the logic.

"Really, Nathan?" she hissed out, nostrils flared. "You really want to talk about what's disrespectful? Why am I here, Nathan? Why am I even here in the first place? You know what? I can't do this with you. Nope." She rushed past me, not looking back.

"Naomi, Naomi!" I called after her as my eyes peered around.

"Nathan, stop harassing my guest; your kids are ready to go, man!" Tess yelled.

I hated that woman; I really did. I seethed as my eyes moved past her to see Teddy's big ass move into view again. *What man really wants to be that big? Over there, looking like a black Incredible Hulk, I bet he's as dumb as rocks.*

As if reading my mind, he winked, smiling wide. He moved in front of Tess, cutting off my view from the wicked witch of the West. He picked her up like she weighed nothing and held her under her butt. The way they looked at each other made me want to throw up. *Yep, definitely time to go.*

"Okay, Daddy, we're ready," Nya informed.

I turned around to see my three blessings heading my way. "Nate, grab Livy's overnight bag, and I will hold yours and Nya's.

"Okay, Daddy!" he said excitedly. "We're gonna have some fun!" he yelled, hurrying to do as I asked. My eyes roamed to Naomi, laughing at something Terrell had said. Instantly seeing red, I debated if I should go over there to remind her that we were still married. This shit was unacceptable; if she was going to be here, she better stop talking to all these me—

"Daddy, we're ready." I heard Nya say, this time all her patience gone, pulling me from my spiraling thoughts.

I released a heavy sigh. "Okay, babies, let's go."

～

Naomi

Later that night after everyone had left, I laid in bed as my mind replayed the day. I tried to relax, but knowing Nathan would be there filled me with dread. I noticed him as soon as he stepped into the backyard. It had been such a wonderful party before he showed up. Tess did an amazing job. She went with a Black Panther-themed party that appealed to everybody. Nate Jr. and his little friends could be a rowdy bunch, while Nya and her squad were little divas in the making. But Tess made it all work.

While I scanned the backyard, I watched all the little T'Challa's and Shuri's running around having the time of their lives. I remember thinking how I wasn't ready to confront Nathan.

"Hey Nay, can I sit with you?"

I heard someone ask before I turned to see Rob's handsome face staring down at me.

"Sure," I told him, happy for the distraction.

"How are you holding up?" he asked, looking at my hands as I played with my bracelets. "Those are nice, one on each wrist like Wonder Woman."

I laughed. "Thanks, they were a gift to myself."

"That's cool; you should always celebrate yourself. My sister celebrates herself a little too much, going by Teddy's reaction when he gets her credit card statement." He shook his head with a laugh.

After releasing a heavy sigh, I told him what was bothering me.

"I thought I was ready to see him, but now, I'm unsure. I'm just so angry with his sorry ass; I don't want to make a scene today."

"Well, if you make one, we got your back and would look the other way if you went upside his head," he said with a playful grin on his lips.

"Stop, there is no way I would get physical with children around; who would do something like that?"

"Uh, have you not met my sister?" He laughed at my expression. "Stick around long enough; I promise you will get to witness Miss Saditty show her ass."

I burst out laughing. Tess could be something else. I'd observed her with her clients. She was always so compassionate and professional; I knew there was another side to her.

Right at that moment, I heard Nathan ask, "Naomi, can I speak to you?"

I didn't want to make a scene in front of Rob, so I walked over to a corner to give us some privacy. Of course, it didn't take Nathan long to piss me off; after hearing his insult, I walked off.

I laid there, trying to decipher my feelings. I loved my husband, but I didn't know if we could get past this. Maybe it was my fault. Maybe he needed something I wasn't giving him.

As fast as the thought entered my mind, I shot it down.

Nope ... we're not going down that road, Naomi. If that were the case, I was his wife, and he should have come to me. I refused to take the blame for this. I would have gladly done whatever it took to make things right; he didn't give me that chance. *So, I'm going to take my time to decide what I want to do, whether he likes it or not.*

CHAPTER SEVEN

Naomi

Early the next morning, I was woken up by my cell vibrating against the nightstand. Not ready to wake up, I rolled over, letting the call go to voicemail. When the phone didn't ring again, I figured it wasn't that important and decided to check the message when I got up.

Wait a minute. The kids aren't in the other room sleeping. They went with Nathan last night. What if something happened? Now wide awake, I fought with the covers that had me wrapped tight in a cocoon.

When I was free, I grabbed my cell and saw a missed call from my mother. Relief briefly flooded my system.

When was the last time I spoke to anyone in my family? When did anyone last call to check in to see how Livy and I were doing?

I leaned against the headboard and tried getting comfortable, deciding to call her back. I blew out a puff of air and hit talk.

She picked up on the first ring.

"Hello Naomi. How are you?"

"I'm good; how are you, Mom? Is everything okay?"

"Why wouldn't it be, dear? Kenny and Zena have never given me an ounce of trouble. You're the only one of my children that's ever caused me any grief, but you're out in Texas, so I'm carefree.

"Mom, that was unnecessary," I said, rubbing my eyes.

"Oh, stop, Naomi, I was kidding. Everything's fine here; I was calling to see if you were coming home for your brother's wedding?"

"Of course, I will be there. But why is this the first time I'm hearing about Kenny getting married? No one thought to call and tell me?"

"Naomi, with you living in Texas, you miss out on a lot of family news."

"I'm a phone call away, Mom; you could have called."

"Naomi, I'm not going to sit here and do this with you today; I have a lot to do. I will make sure you receive an invite. I have to go; your father is calling me."

I can't even say I'm shocked by that call. I'm used to it at this point. Sadly, I needed this call today. I'd been going back and forth on whether to stay in Texas or return to California.

My parents always showed me that things were always my fault or could have been avoided had I not done this or that.

Whatever.

After my morning meditation, I went into the bathroom to start my day. As I brushed my teeth, I continued to think about my dilemma. *Can I move back to California if Nathan and I can't work things out?* I didn't know how receptive my family would be to my baby. I would hope they wouldn't take how they felt about me out on their grandchild, but with my parents, you never knew, and that was a risk I wasn't willing to take. If they ever made Livy feel something was wrong with her for any reason, I wasn't sure what I would do. I sighed hopelessly, walking out of the bathroom and into my closet to see what I would wear. I paused as memories I kept locked away tried to surface.

"Nope, not today, Satan." I dressed rapidly and headed downstairs.

The house was quiet, letting me know I was the first one up. A smile spread across my face as I hurried toward the kitchen.

She's not going to beat me today. When she came down, I'd have breakfast ready. That woman never slept. She was always the last to go to bed at night and the first one up. But not today, "little miss perfect," I got this.

What the hell was that, *grunting?* I usually heard when Tess or Teddy left their bedroom, so it wasn't them. I proceeded on with caution, craning my neck to find the source. My mouth damn near hit the floor when I found it. On its own accord, my body aligned itself with my head to get a better look. Before me was a shirtless Rob, wearing a pair of the most delicious black exercise shorts I'd ever seen. His broad shoulders filled the doorway as he did pull-ups on a pull bar. I stood there speech-less. The man's body was a work of art.

"I'm sorry, Nay, was I too loud?"

He was facing me with hands on his hips, breathing hard. *Damn it, he caught me staring.*

"Um, no," I told him, trying to stop my eyes from trailing the glistening sweat running down his magnificent chest.

I cleared my throat. "You're fine; I was hoping to beat Tess to the punch and make everybody my irresistibly delicious French toast this morning."

"Uh-oh," he said with a laugh.

"What do you mean uh-oh?" I asked, proud of myself for stopping my wayward eyes. "Do you think she would mind? She rarely sleeps in, so I figured I would help her out this morning."

"No, she won't mind. She's just bossy and doesn't like to give up control. Tell you what, let me fold up my blankets and shower, and I will help you."

"You don't have to do that; I got this."

"I know you do, but I want to help," he beamed, "give me a few minutes, and I will meet you in the kitchen."

He reached up to release his pull-up bar before entering the den.

"Well, I had a sous chef whether I wanted one or not," I murmured as I walked into the kitchen.

"Damn, that smells good already. Where do you want me?" Rob's deep voice inquired as he walked into the kitchen.

I paused whisking the eggs, vanilla extract, and cinnamon in a shallow dish.

"Um, you can start by cutting up some fruit over there." I pointed with my elbow toward the bowl of fruit on the island.

"Come on; I can help with more than cutting up the fruit."

"Oh yeah?" I asked, trying not to laugh as I stirred in some milk.

"Yeah, whatever you need, I'm sure, I can handle it."

I peered at him over my shoulder, eyeing him as he pulled his lower lip between his teeth.

"I'm sure you can, but I've got everything covered except the fruit." I smiled and turned back around.

As we worked in silence, I placed a skillet on the stove and walked to the pantry to grab a new jar of coconut oil. I glanced over to see Rob cutting up the pineapple. I returned to the counter, trying to unscrew the lid. After several unsuccessful tries, I put it down and looked for a butter knife to help break the seal.

"Here, why don't you let me help you with that?" he asked, making me jump. He wrapped his arms around me to unscrew the jar. We weren't touching, but he was close enough for me to feel the heat from his body. Being trapped between his large body and the counter, I refused to allow any parts of my body to graze the front of his. I kindly mumbled an *excuse me* and I slipped out the side.

"Yeah, okay," he murmured with a laugh that skirted across my skin.

That man is too damn fine for his own good and my sanity.

After breakfast, everybody remained at the kitchen table. Teddy timed his arrival perfectly, as always. He walked in as we were setting the food on the table.

"That was bomb, Ladybug; if we were at a restaurant, I would have been compelled to leave you a generous tip."

"Don't let that stop you. I don't have a problem taking tips," I told him, holding out my hand. I caught Rob eyeing my shining bracelet from the corner of my eye.

"I just did. I told you everything was delicious; that's got to count for something, right?"

He looked so serious; I had to laugh.

"Well, I cooked too; where's my thanks?" Rob chimed in.

"Boy, Naomi had you cut up some fruit and set the damn table. In my book, that's not cooking." This came from Tess.

"What's everyone's plan for today?" Teddy asked, sipping his coffee.

"Well, I'm meeting with a new client, so I better get ready," Tess said, standing up from the table.

"Thanks, Nay, everything hit the spot," she said as she rushed out.

"What about you, Nay?"

"I planned to paint in the backyard until Nathan dropped the kids off."

"Okay, that sounds fun and relaxing. When are we going to see some of your pieces?" Teddy enquired.

"Soon, hopefully, I didn't think to grab my portfolio when I left home; I wished I had. But you can go on my Instagram page and see some of my work there."

"I will do that," Teddy said with a friendly wink.

"She's amazing. Each of her paintings tells a story."

"You've seen my work?"

I didn't know why I was hit with insecurity; I was proud of my work. Painting started as an outlet for me. My good friend Kirk was the only person to view my work for the longest time. I remembered when he first suggested it was time to share my art with the world.

"Yes, you're amazing; how long have you been painting?" Rob asked.

"For about nine years. A friend introduced me to painting and taught me everything I know," I said with pride.

"Well, maybe you can teach me a few of those techniques," Tee said as he sipped orange juice.

"Poor Livy and Nya wanted me to draw fish the other day. All I had for them was a horizontal figure eight; I erased one end to make a little tail. I made a dot with the pen's tip for the eye and drew a half circle above it for the eyebrow. Hell, they loved it; I just felt it was lacking somehow," he said with mock disappointment.

"No problem, Tee, join me anytime," I told him, laughing as I stood from the table.

That happy, warm feeling was gone when I reached the room. Thinking about the conversation I had with my mother soured my mood. My family and I would not have done this, sitting around the table, laughing, and enjoying life. They would be more concerned if I were going to break down and embarrass them in some way. It would be hell for me to live like that again. *I think I've finally made up my mind.*

CHAPTER EIGHT

Nathan

Why is she continuing to be this difficult? Does she not see how weak this shit makes me look? Does she even care? She had no business running to them. I mean, what kind of woman would do something like that? She could have gone to a hotel, but my ex-wife's house? It's just foul. I know I fucked up, but now she's prolonging this.

"Mr. Wells, Mr. Warren can see you now."

Jarred from my thoughts, I got to my feet to greet Albert's gorgeous secretary.

"Why thank you, beautiful," I told her with a smile as I walked into Albert's office. "She's a beauty, Albert," I told the older, heavyset white man with thinning hair sitting behind the large Brazilian rosewood desk.

"Hey Nate, what brought you all this way?" he asked with a megawatt smile, getting to his feet to shake my hand.

Albert's company was one of my biggest accounts. I always conducted business with his company in person. I'd made a pretty penny off this man and planned to have a long and prosperous future with Warren and Associates.

"I was in the area and figured I would stop in to drop off the life insurance contract," I told him, lifting the folder in my hand.

"You didn't have to inconvenience yourself; I could have sent a courier."

"It's not an inconvenience at all. It's always a pleasure to visit with an old friend."

"Good, good, hey look, I've been meaning to call you." He dropped his voice and leaned in. "I wanted to apologize if I played a part in what went down with your wife," he said while scratching the back of his thick neck.

I sat across from him, not knowing what to say, as my temperature rose.

I can't believe that bitch came back and blabbed what happened.

"Everything is fine; it was all a misunderstanding. Naomi's fine." I covered my lie with a nervous chuckle.

"Wow, that's not what Shelly said; she said when your wife walked in, all hell broke loose."

My laugh sounded false to my ears as I tried to play it off.

"I mean, yeah. It was tense for a moment."

"Shelly said she thought she would lose her life that night. Listen, son." He lowered his voice once more. "When I sent her to you as a thank you for your service and hard work, I uh … didn't think you would take her home, son; I assumed you would have your little rendezvous at a hotel or somewhere private like the rest of us," he told me with a look of annoyance.

"I'm sorry if I overstepped my bounds. Shelly is a party favorite; I only send her when someone has rendered a job well done. She's been with me for a long time, and I trust her discretion. I went on and sent her a handsome bonus to make sure she doesn't share what happened with anyone because if what she knows were ever to get out, let's just say, there would be a lot of financially bleeding businessmen after their wives' divorce lawyers are through with them, mine included. Do you get what I'm saying, son?"

"Ah yes, I believe I do."

"But don't worry about it; as I mentioned, it was handled. I really like you, Nathan, and I look forward to a long business relationship with your company. I hope this won't be a problem. We look down on divorce here. I mean, family in everything, am I right?"

"Yes, sir, you are correct."

"Good, so you and Naomi are good then?"

"Yes, we are; we're better than good. If anything, this has only made us closer." I smiled big.

"Good, because I look forward to your wife and that gorgeous little girl at our upcoming holiday festivities at my home."

"That sounds wonderful. I'm sure Naomi and Livy will love that. Thank you, sir."

"No problem; with that out of the way, let's get down to business, shall we?"

Shit, I got to get my wife back.

CHAPTER NINE

Naomi

"What is up with this man?" I looked down at the screen to see the thirteenth missed call from Nathan. *He has been calling nonstop since yesterday, but I know it's time for us to talk. I've been stalling because I know he isn't going to like what I have to say. I know myself too well to know; I could never get past something like this. The amount of work I've put into to protect my mental health won't allow me to.*

I was sitting there deep in thought when Tess said, "Penny, for your thoughts." I glanced up to see her enter the room.

"It's nothing; what's up with you?" I asked brightly, not ready to share.

"Good, because we're going out tonight with my girls, so wear something cute. Teddy and Rob will be here with the kids while we go shake our asses."

"I can watch the kids while you hang with your girls."

"Why? You don't want to come?" she asked with hurt eyes.

"Tess, you've been amazing since Livy and I have been here. You treat us like family—"

"Because that's exactly what you are, *family*," she huffed out.

"I know you see it that way, and I love you for that, but others may not. The truth of the matter, I am your ex-husband's current wife. Your friends may see me as your enemy like any good friend would. So I will hang out here, but I want you to have fun tonight; I got the kids."

"Girl, girl, girl," Tess said, laughing. "Now you have to come; I can't wait for you to meet Mona and Robyn. I will let them tell you who they are to each other and how they met. So get up, wash your ass, and wear something sexy; we're going out."

I laughed at the silly woman that had walked out the door. I released a sigh and rolled off the bed to get ready.

With Houston's erratic weather and limited clothing options, I chose a pair of black leggings with a black off-the-shoulder top. I found a pair of my cute heels I had left in my car that worked with the outfit. It was a simple yet sexy look, and I felt good. Houston was such a vibrant city that came alive at night. It had a little something for everybody. When we arrived at the club, I noticed two women waving us down; I assumed to be Robyn and Mona.

"Girl, what took you so damn long?" the pretty, short one of the two asked. She had the cutest shape on her petite stature. Her long, blonde wig cascaded down her back.

"You know how traffic can get down here, and you couldn't have waited that long," Tess said, walking up to hug her friends.

"This is my homegirl, Naomi. Nathan's wife."

That made me wince hearing her say that.

"Nice to meet you, Naomi; I love those shoes, girl. I'm Mona and short stack right there is Robyn." She gave me a beautiful smile.

Mona put me in the mind of a dark-skinned Kimora Lee Simmons, with her height and gorgeous exotic look.

"Shut up, Mona, just because I'm not as tall as a giraffe like you, I'm far from short, so get it right."

Why was I the only one shocked to hear how Tess introduced me? Her friends did not bat an eye. *Have things changed that much? Why does all of this seem so normal to everybody but me?*

Tess's laughter cut through my thoughts. "Come on, let's get inside and order some drinks so y'all can tell Naomi how this ghetto-ass friendship came to be. Then maybe she can relax and have a good time."

"Let's go!" Mona yelled, dancing toward the entrance.

Once inside, we made our way over to the bar. The first thing I noticed about the club was that they played *nineties* music, which made my soul happy. I looked around, taking in the beautiful decor. This had to be the cutest bar I'd ever been to, with the different shades of pink throughout. The overhead lighting cast a soft blush glow on everyone, almost giving a filter. *That could be dangerous,* I chuckled. Pink brick walls and rich ruby-red velvet curtains gave it a seductive and inviting vibe.

Now seated at the bar, Tess ordered a couple of shots, setting one in front of me.

"I will need you to have a drink before they start," she shouted over the music as "I Want Her" by Keith Sweat started to play, making me dance in my seat.

"No, thank you, I don't drink," I hollered right back.

She leaned over to say, "Trust me, you're going to need this."

An hour later, I slurred loudly, "Okay, let me get this straight." I looked at Robyn. "You're Charles's son's mother?"

"Yep," was all she said, sipping her drink.

I pointed to Mona. "And you're his girlfriend?"

"I'm trying to be, but if he keeps playing with me, his ass is going to do that time all by himself, and then we'll see if that bitch is going to hold him down," she said, heated.

"Oh, there's another?" I asked, confused again after working hard to keep everything in order.

I was trying my damnedest to keep up with the crazy story. Tess was right, though. Believe it or not, it didn't make sense until after my second shot.

"Mona, stop; you're going to confuse her more. Please explain how this hot ass mess of a friendship came to be." Tess chuckled.

"I'll start," Robyn said, turning to me.

"I owned a hair salon I opened with my son's father some years ago. It worked because I was a stylist, and he was a barber. Charles was the perfect gentleman. He was always on his best behavior. Never once did I catch him looking at any of my clients. Everything was going great."

She paused to take a generous sip of her drink.

"So we went to Las Vegas one year to celebrate the salon's success. We ended up off the strip at this jewelry shop with all these unique pieces—the kind of jewelry you wouldn't find anyone else wearing. I fell in love with these two stunning dragon bypass rings with blue sapphire eyes. I had once read that a dragon is a well-known fortune symbol. So I was like, babe, we have to get these! I slid mine on my ring finger, and his went on his pinky. I remember him saying, 'This is the first of many, baby girl, watch.'" She rolled her eyes with a laugh.

"Fast forward a couple of years, and we now have two locations—one for the barber shop and one for the hair salon. One Saturday, I had an appointment with a girl named Mona and two of her friends. When miss thang walked in—"

Robyn paused to look over at Mona before she playfully rolled her eyes.

"I had her sit with my washer to get her started. As I was doing my thing, I overheard my assistant Renee say, 'That's a pretty ring; my boss has one similar.' I didn't trip on the comment because I tend to mind the business that pays me. But I picked up on Mona talking about her dude to her friends; she was saying Charlie this and Charlie that.

"I was still not thinking much of it because, mind you, I've never called Charles anything other than Charles. So when it was time for Mona to sit in my chair, I finally caught a glimpse of the ring on her finger ..."

Mona chimed in at this point.

"She was like, 'Please tell me where you got that ring, and I advise you not to lie.' I said, 'Girl, lie for what?' I proceeded to tell her it belonged to my man. He had left it on my nightstand.

"'Charlie right, that's your man?' Robyn asked as she brought her hand up to show me the exact ring that sat on her finger. Now, you probably think we lit into each other, right? Not-at-all. She asked if we could go and talk in her office. My friends questioned my sanity, but I was interested in hearing what she had to say. So we sat and talked and confirmed Charlie was, in fact, Charles and was a no good cheating bastard."

They were both sitting here and able to laugh about it now; I hoped they left Charlie/Charlie's ass for dead.

I noticed Mona looked down at her hands; *uh-oh.*

"Well, Robyn was smarter than me. She wouldn't forgive him for cheating, and they parted ways. He kept the barbershop, and she kept the salon and went on to open two more," she said with pride, looking at her friend. "I, on the other hand, felt bad after he gave me a sob story about a broken childhood. I myself had a broken childhood Not too long after that, he got caught up in illegal activity surrounding his shop, which landed him in jail. I've been supporting him since he's been down."

"You deserve so much more, Mo," Robyn said sadly.

"Girl, stop, enough of that," she said with a wave of her hand. "Right now, let's show Naomi a good time." She drank the rest of her tequila as she got to her feet.

"Let's go, ladies," she said as she danced her way to the dance floor.

I was unsure how I felt about that crazy story or their friendship, but who was I to say who should and shouldn't be friends? I downed the rest of my tequila and followed her to the dance floor as Bell Biv DeVoe's "Poison" started to play.

~

"Here, drink this," I told Tess, handing her a green smoothie. "It will help rid our bodies of the toxins from all the alcohol we drank last night."

"Um … no thanks," she said, eyeing the green liquid skeptically. "All I need is a couple of cups of hot tea, and I'll be good as new."

"How in the world can you be married to *Zeus, king of the gods,* and swear you're 'vegetable juice intolerant'? Is that even a thing?" I asked, giggling.

"First, it is definitely a thing, and did you enjoy yourself last night?" she asked with a huge smile.

"I did! I enjoyed meeting Robyn and Mona," I told her, walking over to the papasan chair in the corner of the room.

"They have no sense whatsoever but have hearts as good as gold. After hearing how their friendship came to be, I hope you can relax being here."

"Um, Tess, in case you haven't noticed. I *am* relaxed being here. Maybe a little too relaxed." I tucked my feet under me to get more comfortable.

"And the sad part is Charles or Charlie ain't even that cute," she said with a face. "See, that is our problem. As women, we *must* see our self-worth; we can't wait for a man to give us that. A real man wants to enhance what's already there; a no-good dirty dick bastard wants to plant doubt. To make you second guess yourself and start viewing his sorry ass as the prize. I had to learn that the hard way."

That caught me by surprise. Tess exuded confidence.

"Yes girl, I've been through some things too. I've had men constantly tell me how strong-willed and opinionated I was. I've always known what I did and didn't like. I never understood why someone wouldn't voice what they truly felt. Anyway, after a while, I began to think maybe I was too opinionated and started to second-guess myself. Could you believe there was a short time in my life I actually turned into a 'yes woman'?"

No, I couldn't believe that, nor did I want to. To think she once allowed a man to make her want to change who she was, didn't sit right in my spirit.

"Girl, stop with the sad eyes, as you can clearly see, it didn't stick. It was way too exhausting, always trying to suppress who I was. I learned Tessa Alexandria may not be perfect, but I have a good heart and I'm a good woman. Plus, my mama always told me, 'Never change who you are for a man, Tessa be loud and proud.' Enough about me, tell me something about you, about your family?" she asked, tilting her head.

For a second, I sat quiet and thought about home. If I'd packed Livy up and returned to California, my family wouldn't have kind words for me like Tess's mother offered. No, to my parents, I would be called unstable and unable to cope with what life has dealt me. They wouldn't praise the bigger picture and see how far I'd come. I would have a daily reminder that I couldn't cope. If I had to deal with that on a daily basis, it would most likely land me back in the hospital. I refused to allow that to happen for any reason.

I'd have to find my way and make it work here in Texas. After all, I had Livy to think about. I'd worked hard to get to this place. It was time for me to prove that I can live this life on my own terms.

Tess's friends made me rethink my current situation. Life

sometimes gets complicated. You have to look past what others consider "normal" and do your own thing and make your own way despite how that may look to others.

"You good girl, why did you get so quiet?"

"I was thinking, no matter what happens, I've decided, Texas is my home now."

"Glad to hear it because we're going to tear some shit up."

God help us.

CHAPTER TEN

Naomi

"Hi Naomi, can I paint with you?"

Nate Jr. asked one day when I was in the backyard getting ready to paint.

"Of course, you can; I would love for you to join me. Sit right here and let me get you set up."

He bounced across the lawn to do as I asked. He was a beautiful mix between his mother and father. He had Nathan's hazel eyes, light-brown skin tone, and black curly hair, like Livy's, and his mother's full lips and long eyelashes.

Once I had him all set up, I surveyed as he made a few false starts, unsure how to begin.

"You know what I like to do before I get started?" I asked.

"What?"

"I first close my eyes. I take a few deep breaths and think about the last interesting thing I saw. I try to think about how it made me feel. After that, I open my eyes, grab my pencil, and sketch what I see in my mind's eye to the best of my ability. It doesn't have to be perfect; it helps to get the idea out of my head and onto paper. Try it with me; close your eyes and take some deep breaths.

As he did as I asked, I continued giving him instructions. "Okay now, think about that thing that called to you, and try to remember how it made you feel."

I caught a shadow passing by the backdoor. I glanced in the direction to see if anyone had come out here.

I turned back to my canvas, picked up a pencil, and sketched out a cute little Pomeranian I saw on my walk the other day. He was the cutest little thing. Once I got Livy and me settled somewhere, I'd get a dog.

When I finished with my sketch, I asked, "So, what do you think?"

"Hm, not bad, not bad at all," he stated, inspecting my sketch, stroking his chin while turning his head this way, then the other.

The boy was a mess, I noted with a chuckle.

"Okay, Mr. Wells, it's your turn; let's sketch that picture."

About forty-five minutes in, Nate Jr. and I were so engrossed in our sketch that we both jumped when we heard Tess's voice from behind.

"Baby, that's beautiful! I didn't know you were so talented," she exclaimed, coming over to get a closer look as she dropped a kiss on the back of his head.

I glanced over, thoroughly impressed. He drew a lion's head. It was very detailed in its simplicity.

"Thanks, mama. It's Naomi; she made this so much fun. Can we do this again soon?" he asked with hopeful eyes.

"We sure can; I would love the company."

"Yes! Will it be alright if I go show Papa Teddy my lion?"

"Of course, here, let me get it down for you." After I released the picture from the makeshift easel, I carefully gave it to him. "Here you go, kiddo. I will let you know when we can do this again; I promise it won't be too long.

"Thank you, Naomi."

He kissed my cheek before running off.

I watched him go as he scrambled inside the house.

"Girl, I don't know why you're acting so shocked; you know my son adores you."

While putting my materials away, I decided to ask her something that's been on my mind.

"Tess, I wanted to ask you, why is Rob single? He and Terrell are wonderful men; why don't they have girlfriends?"

She laughed while saying, "Girl, Terrell is simple. He's too much of a man whore to settle down with one woman."

"That sounds about right," I said with a smirk. The man flirted shamelessly with women everywhere we went. She went quiet for a minute. "Tess, I'm sorry I'm not trying to pry; that was rude."

"Girl, relax; I was wondering where I should start. You see, Rob was in a relationship with a woman named Brie for about four years. Everyone assumed they were going to get married," she said with an eye roll. "They seemed deliriously happy, but I noticed everything changed when Brie got pregnant. I could tell my brother was over the moon about becoming a father, but the further along Brie got, the rockier their relationship became. Rob confided in me to see if he was doing something wrong. He thought maybe he wasn't attentive enough or wasn't listening. I couldn't see anything; all I witnessed was a man deeply in love waiting for the love of his life to have their little bundle of joy."

She paused to release a heavy sigh as sadness clouded her pretty face.

"One evening, Rob came over so distraught I thought I would have to take him to the hospital. He hadn't heard anything from Brie for three days. Then, out of the blue, she sent a random text telling him she wasn't ready to be someone's mother. She said she had been staying with a friend recovering from an abortion. She knew if she had told him about wanting an abortion, he would have tried to talk her out of it, or worse, made her miss the appointment, something she couldn't afford to do because it was so late in the pregnancy already. It was her last chance to have it performed legally. She went on to say, she thought it best for them to take a break to process everything. She apologized for hurting him, but it was ultimately her decision."

Tess sat quietly, worrying her lower lip, staring at the Pomeranian I drew.

"I really couldn't fault her on that because she was correct, but I couldn't get over why go through the motions, making him think she was happy about the pregnancy. They had picked out the theme for the nursery that Rob started working on whenever he was off. Teddy and Terrell chipped in to help build the bathroom. Everybody was excited."

It took a lot to retell the story; I didn't miss the soft sigh that left her lips.

"Naomi, my poor brother was beside himself with grief. I swear I had contemplated murder a few times. We stayed by his side until he slowly emerged from that dark place … but my brother was different. He was harder, colder. That woman broke something deep inside of him. I pray he finds happiness and won't let what happened poison his future. Hearing him say he was done with relationships broke my heart. That coming from Terrell was understandable because he tells every woman upfront he doesn't do relationships, and they still choose to mess with him. Hearing that from Rob, I knew it was coming from a hurt place."

After talking to Tess, I reflected on the times I caught a sad expression cross Rob's handsome face and how he sometimes went quiet when he thought no one was watching. I wondered if he was thinking about the child he never got the chance to meet. I also noticed that if Terrell was around, he didn't let his friend remain quiet or withdrawn for too long.

They have both brought me so much comfort during this crazy time in my life. Now, after hearing about what Rob went through, I wanted them to know I'm also there for them.

It's funny how life can change so drastically in such a short period.

CHAPTER ELEVEN

Naomi

"It's time for us to talk, Naomi."

That was the last voicemail I had received from Nathan from a few days ago when Tess and I went out with her friends. He gave it a break because he'd been silent since. But he was right; it was time for us to talk.

Sitting at the kitchen table, I sighed and closed my eyes. My time was up. I'd had the freedom to do some soul-searching. The truth was, I loved my husband, but could I move past the fact he slept with another woman? We could try marriage counseling and put in the work to fix what was broken, but the more I thought about it, I didn't know if I wanted to invest the time and the work. I felt like I would be taking a huge step back. I'd worked hard to get where I was. I would have to deal with insecurity constantly and wonder if he was out somewhere cheating whenever he came home late from work—the constant tasting his words for lies. There was no way my mental health wouldn't suffer from that. It was now clear to me that moving back to

California was no longer an option. Texas was my home now. *I don't know how I will work it out, but I've decided.*

I blew out a cleansing breath and sent Nathan a text, letting him know I was ready to talk.

CHAPTER TWELVE

Naomi

"Livy, stop running; how many times do I have to tell you to *walk*."

"I'm sorry, Mommy, I will walk," she said in that little voice of hers, making me smile.

My daughter always scared me with her run when she was excited about something.

"Good, once you have your swimsuit on, you can join us in the back. Remember to walk, alright."

"Nate Dog! We are here. Are you ready?"

I looked over to see Terrell and Rob come through the front door.

"Yes, let me grab my basketball!" Nate Jr. called out, unable to get to his feet fast enough.

"How you doin', Sister-in-law?" Terrell said to Tess pulling her in for a quick hug. "Hey, Ladybug, do you want to shoot some hoops with us at the park?" he asked, looking over at me.

"That sounds like fun, but Tess and I were going to spend some time with the girls in the pool."

"I got the ball! Let's go!" Nate Jr. yelled as he burrowed past us right out the front door.

"Have fun swimming," Rob said with a smile as he and Terrell hurried out to catch up with a deliriously happy Nate Jr.

I hadn't realized I was staring at the door until Tess said, "Um, are you ready, girl?" My cheeks got hot as I rolled my eyes and walked past her. "I don't know why you are marching off like that. I wasn't the one gazing at a closed door." She continued to laugh, which only made my embarrassment worse.

When I turned around to tell her nobody was gazing, Livy's tiny feet running upstairs again distracted me. "Livy, stop—"

I didn't get the chance to finish before her scream pierced the air.

I reached the bottom of the stairs, where my baby lay broken and unconscious.

Oh god.

CHAPTER THIRTEEN

Act 2
Houston Methodist

Naomi

"You were probably too busy laughing and giggling with your 'new friends' than watching our daughter. She got hurt on your watch, Naomi. None of this would have happened if she had been home like she should have been. I hope you realize this is your fault."

"Back off, Nathan," Tess said angrily.

"Tess, please stay out of this. It's between me and my wife."

"That's fine, but you yelling at her doesn't help the situation. She's been through enough tonight; everyone's main concern should be on Livy now."

"Can you please get your wife?" He looked over at Teddy for help.

Teddy ignored him as he kissed Tess's cheek. "I'm going to go call and check on the kids. I will let your mother know we will probably be here for a few more hours. I'll be right back."

"Rob?" Teddy called out.

"I'm here. Don't worry; I'm not going anywhere," he said as he and Terrell made it over to us.

"Cool, I'll bring you and Naomi back some hot coffee," Teddy said to his wife.

"Thank you, baby," Tess said after her thoughtful husband.

"Why are y'all even here?" Nathan started while turning and looking around at everyone.

"The only people that need to be here are Naomi and me. I appreciate you all being here, but you can go now," he said dismissively.

All ignored him as Tess hugged me and said, "Don't worry, she will be okay."

"This shit is just weird," Nathan stated, watching us before he stormed off.

"Why is it so hard for him to understand we're friends?" I asked, watching Nathan down the hall. I looked back at Tess. "Are you sure it isn't written someplace we aren't supposed to be?" I finished with a watery chuckle.

"Girl, please. Says who? That bozo? You're a good person Naomi, and everybody knows I'm fly, don't let what Nathan says get under your skin. Love can be found in the most unlikeliest places, so can friendships. I feel blessed to have you and Livy in my life. You and I don't have to be enemies just because I'm … Nathan's ex-wife," she struggled out. "Clearly, we both had a lapse in judgment," she said making me smile. "Now come on, let's go check on our girl."

Later that evening, we learned Livy had broken her right femur and sprained her wrist. The doctors assured us that young children are resilient and expected her to recover fully. Because the fall knocked her unconscious, they wanted to monitor her for two days. My eyes were almost swollen shut from all the crying.

"Are you sure you don't want me to stay here with you and Livy tonight?"

"No, Tess, you've been here long enough, and I'm sure the kids are worried sick about their sister and ready to go home. Go reassure them that Livy will be fine."

"Okay," she said reluctantly, "but call me if you need anything or us to come back up here, okay?

"I will."

I watched them gather their things when I heard, "Naomi?" I turned to see Rob offering a kind smile.

"Listen, I will be starting my shift soon; I will be right upstairs on the third floor; I will come and check on you both on my b—"

"Thanks, Rob, but that won't be necessary," Nathan chimed in, walking up beside me.

I could tell Rob wanted to say more but decided against it. He turned and walked away.

I watched them make their way toward the exit. The farther they got, the lonelier I felt, even though Nathan stood beside me. I couldn't help the feeling of loneliness seeping in.

A couple days later, when Livy was to be released, her doctor ordered another X-ray to ensure her femur was set properly. When the doctor walked into the room with a somber expression, I knew I wouldn't like what she had to say.

"Hey, everybody," she said, taking us all in. Seeing three huge men and Nathan stuffed in this tiny room must have been a sight to see. "I see Ms. Livy has quite the tribe; that's great, I love to see it." She chuckled. "For those of you that haven't met me yet, I'm Dr. Sharice Milum, an orthopedic surgeon here at Houston Methodist."

Dr. Milum was a beautiful older woman in her late fifties with milk chocolate skin and gray dreadlocks that hung down her back. Even though her words were kind, she demanded your attention with her laser-sharp stare.

With a sigh, she began. "I was hoping we could manipulate the bone without going in because it looked like a clean break, but as the X-ray shows, there's some splintering of the bone. Since Livy is so young and still has much growing to do, I think it would be best to go in and reset the bone. She will need extensive physical therapy. I recommend two days a week for three months once the cast is off. I know it may be overkill, but if that little girl wants to become a world-class ballerina some-day, that's exactly what she will do, and I will make sure of it. But it's your call, Mom and Dad."

"Do you really think surgery is necessary?" Nathan asked.

"For the best outcome, yes. Even though I would like for Livy to have her physical therapy here with therapists I know personally and work with, I see this is far from where you live. We do have physical therapists that could come out to your home, but—"

"Great, that's what we will do," Nathan chimed in.

"Thank you, Dr. Milum, for letting us know our options," I told her.

As soon as she mentioned surgery, my tears began to fall. As I listened, I gave up trying to wipe them away. Someone softly dabbed my cheeks with a napkin. I looked up to see Rob.

"Thanks," I whispered, refocusing on the doctor.

Terrell gave my shoulder a comforting squeeze as Teddy took notes of what the doctor was saying in the corner. Tess had an appointment with a client that was moving out of state, so she couldn't be there. But she made sure Teddy and Rob were here for support, and of course, Terrell wouldn't be left out. I glanced over to catch a look at Nathan's face I'd never seen. I didn't have the mental capacity to try and decipher it, so I listened intently to every word Dr. Milum was saying and when surgery was scheduled.

Nathan

Motherfucker, I fumed. *If not one, it's all these motherfuckers here at any given time. I know this is Tess's meddling ass's doing. This would have been the perfect opportunity to work on Naomi. But that's okay. Now that Livy will have surgery and weeks of physical therapy, they must come home.*

CHAPTER FOURTEEN

Sports bar

Rob

"I swear that dude is mental. I don't know how any woman can stomach him for any time," I told Terrell, releasing a frustrated sigh. "I remember feeling the same way when Tess was with him. And it's sad because Naomi deserves so much better." I paused to bite into my pastrami sandwich.

"Oh yeah? Someone like you, maybe?" he asked, taking a huge bite out of his BLT.

"Ha ha, real funny, man. Stop playing; you know that's not my thing." I drank my iced tea, when a sobering thought occurred. "Hell, if it wasn't for you, Tee, I don't know, man." I rubbed the back of my neck. "I was in a bad place after that shit went down with Brie. I was so looking forward to being a father, man," I told him slowly, looking down.

"I know you were," Terrell said, no longer thinking about his sandwich.

I don't know what possessed me to talk about this right now, but now that I've started, I can't stop.

"And how she took that from me so callously ... hurt like hell. Why wait until she was almost twenty-three weeks to have an abortion? I messed up her little surprise, so I know she wanted that baby too."

"What surprise?"

"Man, I found the sonogram picture in a card that read, 'Surprise, you're going to be a daddy!' in her glove compartment. Whenever I had to go out of town for work, I would take her car and fill it up with gas, so she wouldn't have to worry about it while I was gone. After I pulled her car back into the garage, I figured I would place her key fob inside her glove compartment so that I could hop in my ride and head to the airport. When I looked inside and saw the card, I broke down. I didn't know I wanted to be a father until I looked at my baby in that picture, and she took that from me," I whispered.

"I'm sorry, Rob. I swear, if she were a dude, I would have been fucked her up for you, man. All that I can say is that it's a good thing you found out what type of broad she was before you were tied to her for the rest of your life."

Terrell, being Terrell, offered comfort the only way he knew how: violence.

"You and Teddy are all I have in this world that I care about. It hurt me to my core to see you hurting like that." He was quiet for a minute. "You know, Naomi is amazing—"

"Let me stop you right there, Tee. It's not even like that with me and Nay, I could say the same to you. You need a good woman in your life; maybe you and she could—"

"Ah ah ah," he said with a finger, making me laugh. "We both know, the idea of settling down with one woman gives me hives. Naomi is wonderful and funny as hell, but I feel the same about her as I do about Tess. It's wild because I see her as family in this short time knowing her. On top of that, I'm very fond of my alphabet system. It took me years to cultivate it," he finished proudly.

"Can you share how that works again?" I asked with a sly grin.

"Sure," he said as he wiped his hands on a napkin, leaning forward with excitement. "If I'm out in Cali, it's my goal to find me a Cassie or Celina. If I'm sliding through Tennessee, I'm on the hunt for a Tasha or Tracy, and once I touch down in Florida, I'm looking for a—"

"I got it; I got it; you would be looking for a Faith or a Fallon; I get it, man," I told him, laughing.

"I don't know what you find funny; it definitely keeps shit interesting."

"I bet it does, man."

"Now, can you say the same thing? Do you see Ladybug only as family the way I do?" he asked with a knowing stare, waiting for my answer.

"Shut up, man," I told him, standing. "Let's get back to the gym to help Teddy before his big ass kicks our ass."

"Shit, I don't know what you're talking about; we're big too."

"Yeah, but not bigger than his Mr. Olympian head ass," I told him, laughing as we headed out of our favorite sports bar.

I didn't mention this to Terrell, but I'd been thinking more about Naomi than I care to admit. I had no business being with any woman right now. Especially one that was already going through something with a dirty-ass husband. If she ultimately decided to stay with Nathan or divorced his cheating ass, I could only offer Naomi friendship.

CHAPTER FIFTEEN

Naomi

Livy's surgery was uneventful; she was now awake and back to my old funny baby girl.

"Mommy, when are Nya and Nate going to be here? I want to show them how this works." she asked me while pushing the button to make the bed recline. "Oooh, do you think we could all fit?"

"Girl, you're lying there with a cast up to your thigh, and that bed isn't a ride." I chuckled. I heard children and Tess outside the door, making my heart swell.

"Both of you, act like you have some sense in here; your sister had surgery."

"We will, mama," Nya said excitedly; of course, Nate Jr. remained silent, not subscribing to that. I couldn't help but laugh; I'd missed my buddy.

～

"Are you sure you don't want to stay with us while Livy's healing? You know it wouldn't be a problem whatsoever," Tess asked, sitting on the bed, watching me pack.

When did I buy all of this stuff? I looked down at all the clothes I'd accumulated while staying here.

"I know Tess, and thank you for the offer, but I think a little apartment of my own would be good for me right now. But look how close we will live now!" I squealed.

"I know!" she screamed back.

"Tell me, how did Nathan take it when you told him you were getting your own place?" she asked dryly.

"Well, I haven't told him yet, but I did call him, and we're supposed to meet up this evening to talk."

"Uh-oh, I have an appointment with a new client this evening; how about we meet up with the girls for a drink? You can tell me about the huge hissy fit he is bound to have tonight, embarrassing you both." Her phone started to ring. She glanced down before getting to her feet. "I have to take this; it's one of my clients; I will see you later, okay." She hurried out.

I wouldn't say I was nervous about tonight; I didn't want this to turn into a fight. I'd try my best to show him that it was actually best to have an apartment this close to the rehabilitation center. He also needed to know how much Livy loved being this close to her brother and sister. If he still had a problem, I'd hit him with Houston was much closer than California. We still had a lot to work through, but at least we were still in the same state. He would be able to see his daughter whenever he liked. Livy wouldn't have to split her time between two different states, which meant less travel for everyone. Surely, he could appreciate that.

Once I'd explained all those pros, he had to see this is what was best for everyone. Right?

Feeling good about my plan, I walked into the closet to grab more things to pack.

~

"You did what, Naomi!? How in the hell did you rent an apartment without running it by me first? We are still married, or have you forgotten that fact? I mean, I can see how it could have slipped your mind, being that you're always hanging out over at your sister wife's house," he said with disgust.

"Nathan, lower your voice," I murmured harshly, glancing around the restaurant to ensure he wasn't making a scene.

"It's time for this to stop and for you and Livy to come home. She needs her mother and father more than ever right now. You've been over there letting my ex-wife pump your head up. I have a question: how will you pay for this little apartment? Last time I checked, you'd been a stay-at-home wife for six years. So tell me, *wife*, who will pay for this apartment? Surely you couldn't have been expecting me to," he said so smugly, I wanted to lean across the table and slap the shit out of him.

I closed my eyes, taking a couple deep breaths to get my anger under control.

"You know what, Nathan, let me clarify something. I don't need nor do I have to ask your permission to do a damn thing. I'm a whole grown woman. I'm also a woman who walked in on her husband with his dick inside another woman. So if anyone is in the wrong here, it's you. So you need to climb your ass down from that high horse you are on. After Livy's accident, I figured *maybe* it would give me enough time and space to see if I could forgive you, but after this conversation, I think I'm ready to give you my answer. I can tell you right now while I'm pissed and emotional or after I've had some distance and maybe enough time to miss your ass. So tell me, Nathan, which would you prefer?"

We sat there glaring at each other; he finally released a reluctant sigh. "Let's always keep the lines of communication open while we live apart. Can we at least do that? And we need to discuss who will and won't be in your apartment Naomi."

"Excuse me, what?"

"I have a right to know who will be inside your home. Especially a home I will be contributing to."

"Oh, okay," I said with a sigh of relief. "Since I don't need your money for my apartment, it's none of your concern who's inside. You have a good day, Nathan." I stood and left.

I slammed the car door closed and threw my purse across the seat. "Damn you, Nathan!" I laid my head back and tried to slow my breathing. I had some money in my savings, but it would quickly run out if I didn't do something.

I sat there watching the cars come and go, thinking about this situation. "That's okay; I know what I'm going to do; I'm going to get a job." After pushing down the self-doubt from being out of the workforce for long, I started my car, trying to hold on to my excitement as I drove to pick up my baby girl.

CHAPTER SIXTEEN

My own space

Naomi

"Ladybug! Where do you want this last box to go?" Terrell's deep voice boomed from down the hall.

"Um, you can drop that one in Livy's room, Tee," I hollered over my shoulder.

"I hope you're planning to feed me after this." He grumbled.

I covered my mouth so that he wouldn't hear me snicker. "Of course, I'm going to feed you, big man. You've worked hard these past few days helping me move; you drove the U-Haul to Austin and back.

"I have, haven't I? You know what, scratch that, I want to get paid for my labor."

"Don't worry; I got you, Tee," I told him, laughing. I'd been on cloud nine since I picked up the keys to this place over a week ago. I couldn't get over how cute it was. It was perfect for me and my little lady. I wondered if it was the space that I loved so much or the fact that it was *my* space. Either way, I was happy.

The day we drove to Austin to pick up my things from the house, I tried to make it as easy as possible for Nathan by bringing people he didn't despise … as much as Teddy, Tess, and Rob. So Terrell drove the U-Haul truck while Mona and I followed behind in my car. It started out pretty tense when we first arrived. An angry Nathan scrutinized our every move as we carried my things out. He did finally relent when he said he was going out and to lock up when I left. I wasn't expecting that from him, but I appreciated it.

Everyone had come by to chip in to help Livy and me get settled. When the furniture arrived, it finally started to feel like home. Nathan refused to come by if anyone other than me and the kids were there. That was difficult for him because someone was always coming and going. Oh well, he was going to have to get used to it. I refused to go out of my way to make his ass more comfortable. His main concern should be Livy, anyway.

Enough of that; I have too much to be grateful for. I gave my head a quick shake and got right back to work. I needed to have everything situated before I started work. The thought of my brand-new job made the biggest smile spread across my lips.

"Uh-oh, I'm going to have to tell Tess you're doing that goofy-ass grin thing again."

"Shut up, Tee. Can a girl be happy?"

I lucked up and got a job at an art gallery downtown. They only needed a receptionist, but that was alright; I planned to be the best, overqualified receptionist they ever had. They were skeptical about hiring me in the beginning. I understood, though, I hadn't worked in a long time, but after showing them my portfolio and I may or may not have name-dropped a dear friend that just so happened to be a famous and well-known artist, they decided to give me a chance. I was so grateful that they did. Being surrounded by beautiful works of art every day was a dream come true for someone like me. It just didn't get any better than that.

"Come on, Tee," I told him, getting to my feet. "Let's go get something to eat. My treat."

"Now you're speaking my love language, Ladybug; let's be out."

That night, I woke up in a cold sweat. I hadn't had a nightmare in so long; I almost forgot how terrifying they were. I sat straight up in bed with my hand on my chest, trying to calm my pounding heart. I dreamed I was back in California, walking through the hallway of my parents' huge house.

"Hello? Mom, Dad, Zena, Kenny, is anybody here?" My voice echoed through the still hall, causing me to jump.

I heard a low hum from behind and I glanced over my shoulder with an escalating sense of foreboding. What I saw made my blood turn to ice.

"No! You cannot have me!" I yelled as I took off, running toward my bedroom. The only place I'd ever felt safe in this house.

Elation rushed through me when I reached the second floor and saw my bedroom door come into view. I was almost there, not slowing to look back; my mind was focused; I was going to make it this time. My hand barely touched the doorknob before I was violently tackled to the ground.

"No!" I screamed sorrowfully, feeling the familiar sense of hopelessness. Its black wispy fingers held me down as they spread and settled inside my chest. It shrouded my mind in total darkness, blocking out any glimmer of light. The hopelessness soon turned to dread, making me fight harder. "No!" I screamed, "You cannot have me. I want to live." I cried over and over, refusing to allow it to settle within me. My silver bracelets began to heat up and glow at my wrists. The harder I fought, the hotter they became, as they burned into my skin. I screamed, trying frantically to rip them off. My bracelets. My daily reminders. I looked at them in horror as they continued to burn deep into my wrists, as an old phantom pain returned. The pain I felt as I slid the …

I jolted straight up in bed with a loud gasp as cold sweat covered me. With my heart pounding, I scanned my wrists to ensure nothing had changed. The searing pain was gone. I rubbed my wrists and dropped my head to my chest. I closed my eyes, and I took deep breaths trying to slow my galloping heart. When I opened them, I could feel the familiar darkness tugging at my psyche.

"No, no, no, please, god, no. Not now," I pleaded as I drew my knees into my chest. I glanced at the clock on my nightstand to see it was 3:20 a.m., which was 1:20 a.m. in California. I reached for my phone and paused. *It's the middle of the night, Naomi; what are you doing? Go back to sleep and call her in the morning at a decent hour.* But I had to make the call; I had too much to lose to allow this to pull me under.

After I dialed the number, I waited.

"Hey Naomi, is everything alright?" I heard Dr. Tracy's groggy voice come through.

"I'm so sorry for calling you at this hour, Dr. Tracy, but … I need to talk. To make sure I'm alright."

"I'm listening, dear. Go on, start from the beginning," she replied alertly.

Over the next hour, I shared everything with my long-time therapist and now good friend: Dr. Tracy. She'd been there to witness me at my lowest and darkest hour. I shared everything starting with Nathan's infidelity. Tears ran down my face when I finished, but I felt lighter.

"You've been through a lot these past couple of months, Naomi. Despite it all, it sounds to me like you've been doing well. You have to allow yourself to feel, and to check in with yourself. Always remember, life is about hills and valleys. It's important to remember that when you're low, or going through something difficult, you have to remember, it's not the end, good times will come again. You will find something to smile about again. But you have to be here to experience that. I'm so happy to hear Livy's doing well and about your apartment and new job! That's exciting stuff; please keep me posted, and call anytime."

"Thank you, Dr. Tracy," I told her on a huge exhale. "I will keep you posted with everything, good night."

The next morning, I woke up with a dull headache from my stressful night. I did my best to shake off the residual unease and scooted out of bed to start my day, making sure to take a little extra care this morning. I meditated, took a nice long shower, and made a wonderful breakfast. Around noon I was tying my shoe when my doorbell rang.

"I'm coming!" I yelled, jogging over to answer it. "Who is it?"

"It's me Nay, open up."

I couldn't help the giddy feeling after hearing Rob's voice.

I opened the door to greet him with a bright smile. "Hey Mr. Mason, what up?" I asked, half expecting to see Terrell's big head look around him. I walked back over to put on my other shoe.

"Tess mentioned this was the time you normally walked around the park. I figured I would tag along if that's alright?"

"I would love the company … I mean if you can keep up." I glanced up with an arched eyebrow.

"I see you got jokes this morning, don't act like you don't see me standing here looking like a whole Mr. Olympian." He raised his arms and flexed his huge guns.

I rolled my eyes and pretended to yawn. "Yeah, okay, next time I see Teddy, I'm telling him you're coming for his title."

I laughed when his smile faltered. Everybody knew Teddy was the man, yet he was so humble. He could be mean as a Bullmastiff, ready to tear into anybody that got out of line, but when it came to his wife, he was a tiny French bulldog that followed everywhere she led. They were so adorable it was almost sickening.

"Alright, Hercules," I huffed out as I got to my feet. "Let's go."

It took us a good fifteen minutes to walk over to Memorial Park. It was a nice breezy day, and the temperature was just right. We walked slowly as I listened to him speak. I loved the excitement in his voice whenever he spoke about his residency and his plans to open his own practice.

"I love that you and Tess chose professions to help people. Are your parents in the medical field as well?" I asked, as I started my "lookout" routine.

"Ah no, our parents own a real estate brokerage, but they have always encouraged us to pursue our dreams." He paused to glance around.

"And what about you, have you always wanted to be an artist?"

I didn't hear his question as I squinted my eyes at a figure leaning over the small bridge. When the person stood, I realized he was only throwing bread down to some ducks. I released a small sigh, before I glanced around once more. I probably looked like a crazy person, but I didn't care about that. When I was released from the psychiatric hospital and started outpatient group therapy with Dr. Tracy, I remembered listening to stories from suicide survivors, that if one person had stopped to ask if they were alright, they probably wouldn't have jumped, stepped out into oncoming traffic, or whatever thing they were attempting to do. Maybe it wouldn't have stopped them from trying again, but that day could have turned them in a whole other direction. So now I made it a point to be on the lookout *just in case*, someone was waiting for that person to intervene. To let them know their life mattered, and that they belonged here.

It dawned on me that Rob was still quiet, waiting for me to answer.

"I'm so sorry Rob, what did you say?" I asked, a little embarrassed.

"Uh Naomi, can you tell me what we should be watching out for? I mean are you expecting us to get jumped?" He chuckled but continued to scan the area.

"No silly, jumped by who, a soccer mom and her homies? I'm on the lookout in case someone may need a little help." I shrugged. "An elderly person may have fallen and could be in distress, this is a park, a kid could get hurt. Or someone could need assurance that everything is going to be okay. You'd be surprised what a little reassurance and kindness could do for someone." I smiled.

"So you're on alert to jump in to help if needed, to be a Good Samaritan, huh?"

"Something like that."

Rob stopped in his tracks and stared at me, making me a little awkward. Finally, he removed his jacket and tucked it inside his bag and squatted down to retie his shoes.

"What are you doing?"

"Well, if something just so happens to jump off, no one's going to say I didn't do my part, to jump in and help. I'm getting ready."

We laughed but I could see he was serious.

As he tied his shoes, he tilted his head up to me, wearing a pensive expression. "You're an extraordinary woman Naomi Wells, don't you ever forget that. Do you hear me?"

"Yeah yeah, I heard you Mr. Mason," I told him, playfully rolling my eyes as I offered my hand to help pull him to his feet.

"So I guess I will see you later at Tess and Teddy's for game night?" Rob asked, finishing his water bottle I'd given him when we made it back from our walk.

"I will definitely be there." I walked him toward the front door.

"I really enjoyed our walk today, Naomi. I'm actually looking forward to doing it again, real soon." He paused, staring at me with something in his beautiful brown eyes. "I'd better get going, I need to go get this stank off of me, before running to the grocery store to pick up chicken wings for tonight." He dropped a peck on my cheek and walked out of the door.

I smiled while closing the door. I leaned my back against it and tried my best to hold on to the good vibes.

Game night

"What's up with you girl, why do you look so drained?" Tess asked as soon as I walked into her kitchen.

"I'm good, maybe a little tired," I told her, setting the snacks down I brought for game night.

She lowered her voice to ask, "Is Nathan bothering you?"

"No, not at the moment, thank god," I said with an eye roll.

"That's good to hear, but what's wrong Nay, I see something in your eyes that I don't like."

"I haven't been sleeping well, but it's getting better."

I trusted Tess and knew that I could share what was going on with me. I'd learned to be selective about who I confided in. My own family viewed me as some crazy person or a burden to them. I wanted to fit in so badly; I learned early to shy away from talking about mental illness. It wasn't until therapy that I learned depression is an illness like any other illness. No one asked to become sick, and it sure as hell didn't make you weak. Like any other illness, depression had to be monitored and maintained. If ignored, it could potentially be deadly.

"Tess, I want to share something with you. I hope it doesn't make you see me differently."

"Hold on, come with me first out on the patio so that we can have some privacy."

I followed her outback, and I walked over to my favorite lounge chair. She closed the door and walked over to sit in the one across from me. With kind eyes, she didn't say a word as she gave me her undivided attention.

"I was diagnosed with clinical depression some years ago." I paused to gauge her reaction. "It was difficult with a family like mine. With overachieving parents and siblings, I was often viewed as lazy or unmotivated to do better. They didn't understand, I was doing the very best I could at the time. It got so bad for me, that when I was twenty-three … I had to seek out medical intervention." That was all I was comfortable with sharing at the moment.

Not missing a beat, she chimed in, "Good. No shame in that. I commend you for doing so, I wish more people would. Please continue."

A smile tugged at the corner of my lips hearing her words.

"I was diagnosed and assigned a wonderful therapist that changed my life. Over time, I got my life back and started to live again. I stopped caring about what my family thought of me and focused on my happiness and well-being."

"Yes girl, I love all of that! But you aren't telling me anything, I already knew you were a tough cookie from the very first time we met. I swear if depression was a person, I would have Teddy kick its ass, but I already know you got this, and if ever you need to talk about anything, and Nay," she paused to make sure she had my undivided attention, "I mean anything, you come to me, I promise we will work it out together, okay?"

"I appreciate that. I want you to know the same goes for you Tess, if you need to talk about anything, call me."

"Thank you for trusting me enough to share your past, and on the behalf of Teddy, Terrell, Rob, Nathan Jr., Nya, and I, you and Livy are a part of our tribe now. If anybody comes for y'all, they have to come for us too." She came over to me, pulling me up from my chair and into a big hug.

"Now come on, let's get ready to win this Spades tournament, and listen, if we start to lose, we need to come up with some 'signals' to give across the table, you hear me," she said, lowering her voice and giving me a wink.

"Tess! We are not going to cheat!" I told her, laughing.

"Shh, I didn't say anything about cheating." She quickly scanned the backyard. "Girl, come on, I see now I have a lot to teach you." She huffed, leading me back inside the house.

This all felt so different. When my family first learned I was clinically depressed, you'd have thought I was given three months to live. They began to treat me as if my life was over. If they only knew, it was just beginning.

CHAPTER SEVENTEEN

Rob

"I'm in trouble, Tess."

"What's wrong?" She paused from rummaging through a drawer to look over at me.

I palmed the back of my neck before jumping right in.

"I'm falling for her."

"For who, Naomi?"

"Yes, who else would I be talking about … sorry, sis," I told her as I dragged my hands down my face. "I've tried to keep it strictly platonic, but it's getting hard. The more I get to know her, the harder I feel myself falling. What should I do? Tess, be real with me?"

"Well, sweetie, I can assure you, you're not going to like what I have to say, but I'm going to say it anyway; you're going to have to back off."

"Huh?" That took me by surprise. "Come on, Tess, it's me, not Terrell. I'm not on some love 'em and leave 'em mess. We all know that's Tee all day. He will tell you himself he's trifling."

"I understand all of that, but Naomi is dealing with a lot right now, and you still haven't dealt with your hurt from Brie."

"Don't start, Tess."

"No, you don't start, you asked for my input, so I'm going to give it," she said sternly, looking like our mother's twin.

"You both are in a fragile place right now; the last thing you both need is to 'trauma bond.' Heal first, *then* see what's there. Do you understand?"

"Yeah, I hear you." I hated to admit she was right.

"Good, I love you both, but what the both of you need more than anything is time. As for Terrell, it's only a matter of time before he meets his match, and I can't wait to witness his takedown," she said with an evil cackle.

"You ain't right, sis," I told her, walking over to kiss her cheek and heading out.

∾

Night at the Rodeo

Naomi

Tonight, we were going to the Houston Rodeo. Tess's entire house was buzzing with excitement. I'd never been to a rodeo. Sadly, growing up in Southern California, the only thing I associated with the word rodeo in it was Rodeo Drive in Beverly Hills. When Teddy and Terrell walked in wearing their rodeo attire, I damn near passed out. With all those muscles on display, cowboy hats, and gleaming belt buckles, they would be a fan favorite with the ladies.

I decided to have some fun with my look tonight and wore a gorgeous, long blonde wig, flat-ironed bone straight, under my cowboy hat. I couldn't stop running my fingers through the silkiness; I loved it. Glancing in the mirror, I reflected on my short hair and what prompted me to cut all my hair in the first place. I used hair and a lot of makeup to hide from the real world for many years. It became my costume. I wanted people to believe I had it all together, but little did the outside world know I was dying inside. My hair was the first thing to go once I began to heal. When I witnessed my family's harsh reaction, my universe was already shifting for the better. They all believed I had gone completely mad. With something as small as cutting my hair off, I didn't know, but I was somehow taking my power back.

I smiled and leaned back, making the hair sway from side to side. The wig didn't feel like I was wearing a costume; it just felt fun, like I wanted to change my look. Nothing more, nothing less. *Let's see if blondes do have more fun.* Feeling good, I walked out of the bathroom and ran right into Nathan.

"I didn't know you were going to the Rodeo."

"Why wouldn't I go? I live in Texas, Nathan."

"For starters, you're not even from Texas; what do you know about rodeos?" he asked snidely.

"You're right, I don't know much, but I plan to find out all I can. I hope Houston is ready for Naomi because she's here to stay." I tipped my hat to him and walked off, putting extra sway in my hips.

"See, I told y'all, didn't I? It was only a matter of time before I rubbed off on her." Tess beamed with pride.

I laughed as I caught movement by the kitchen. I hoped it was Rob; I wanted to show him my outfit.

"Mommy, you look so pretty!" Livy called out to me.

"Thank you, baby," I told her, squatting to talk to her.

"Um, Tess, those boots are bad, girl," I commented as she walked over wearing black and white thigh-high cowboy boots with a black skirt and matching top. That black cowboy hat she was sporting with her golden pixie cut and those Ruby Woo red lips were sexy as hell.

"Thank you, sister wife, ooh, look at you in your rodeo get up. Robyn, you did good by our girl, damn Naomi."

I had to agree I looked good in my brown-and-white cow print jumpsuit that tastefully hugged my curves with my white cowboy hat, white rhinestone cowboy boots, and turquoise accents.

"I hope you're proud of yourself, Tess. No self-respecting woman would think of walking outside in what she's wearing."

"Nathan, I'm almost a hundred percent sure you meant that as an insult, but I could kiss you in the mouth for that compliment. The girl looks damn good, doesn't she?" Tess beamed purposefully, overlooking his salty comment.

"Let's go, kids!" he yelled, walking over to the landing.

"Come on, sister wife, let's get our stuff so we can leave."

I grinned when I saw him cringe at hearing the nickname.

Rob

How was I supposed to keep it together when Naomi was out here looking that damn good? It was all Robyn's fault. I should have expected this when I found out she and Naomi went shopping for the Rodeo. This was Naomi's first time attending the Houston Livestock Show and Rodeo. I wanted to make sure she had a good time. But watching her walk around in that jumpsuit was distracting as hell. I couldn't take my eyes off her.

After we arrived at the Rodeo, I got out of my truck and walked over to where Tess and her gang had parked.

As I got closer, I picked up on Mona mentioning some cowgirls.

"We look like 'The Cowgirls of Color,'" she told Tess.

"I told Teddy about them the other day and how I would love to meet them."

"Ooh, I love them too!" Robyn called out, pulling up in her car.

"How are you in our conversation from inside the car, Robyn? You haven't even parked yet, damn," Tess asked with her hands on her hips.

"Girl, please, it's my superpower," Robin replied, getting out of her car with a shrug. "It was passed down from my great-great-grandmother on my mother's side. As we age, our eyesight may go, we may not be able to make it to the bathroom every single time anymore, and we could even forget our own name, but the hearing can still pick up on a whispered conversation being had from the next room over."

I couldn't help but laugh listening to my sister's crazy friend. No wonder they were friends.

"Come on, everybody let's go in. I want a burger."

"Tess, you can't be serious. We just got here; how are you ready to eat?" Mona asked while straightening her skirt.

When they started to walk inside, I followed behind and froze when my eyes landed on Naomi checking me out. I expected her to look away, but she hit me with the lip bite and a challenging stare.

Wait, what? I laughed as I ran my hand down my mouth. Now, I must be seeing things.

"Come on, Naomi, let's go inside; you have to try one of these famous burgers. Forget what Mona's ass is talking about." I overheard Tess say, breaking the spell. Naomi shook her head and turned to catch up to them. That damn wig looked good as hell on her, but I still preferred her beautiful short hair any day.

I bit my lip as a smile spread, realizing I wasn't the only one affected. *Good to know.* I turned in the opposite direction to find my buddies that would be here from Tennessee.

~

Naomi

What in the hell is that man trying to do to me?

How was I supposed to walk, talk, breathe, and smile while acting normal when he had me over here about to short-circuit?

When we parked and got out of Tess's Jeep, I saw Rob climbing out of his truck. My eyes slowly took him in as he made his way over to us.

"Why don't you look nice, baby brother, don't get in here breaking no hearts, you hear me? Tess scolded playfully.

"You know that's not me, sis. Hey ladies, don't y'all look lovely."

He looked at me, tipping his black cowboy hat. "Naomi."

All I could do was stand there, smiling like an idiot.

"Well, I'm going to look for my boys; I will catch up with y'all later to check on you. Have fun."

He turned to leave when Tess said playfully, "Tell Teddy I'm grown and have been grown for a long time."

"You take that up with your husband when you see him. I ain't got nothing to do with that, sis." He winked and turned to leave.

Damn, he looked good. My eyes tracked every move the man made. He looked like a sexy ass black cowboy in all that black.

When he turned back to see me staring, I arched one eyebrow as if to say, *you caught me,* but I didn't look away. *Damn, where did that come from?*

Stop playing with fire, Naomi. I looked up to see Tess *watching.* Feeling like a child caught being fast by her mama, I hurried over with my head down, trying not to look in her face. She didn't say a word, but I could see the laughter in her eyes.

Sometimes I can't stand her.

As we made our way around the Rodeo, I took in all the smiling faces, proudly wearing their Rodeo attire. I met families that had been attending the Rodeo for generations. From the barbecue contests to the music, I'd never experienced anything like it. When I was growing up, I always wished I had grandparents that lived in the Deep South to visit as some of my friends had. The stories they would come back sharing after summer vacation left me feeling empty, like I was missing a part of me.

When we returned to Tess's house, I wasn't as cute as I was when we first left. It was one of the best times I'd had in a very long time. I bought cowboy hats from a vendor for Livy and my sister Zena. I'd keep it for her if she ever visited Texas. I was too tired to drive home, so I stayed in the guest room. After taking off my clothes and taking a hot shower, I passed out with a huge smile on my face.

CHAPTER EIGHTEEN

Rob

"Why can't I get that woman out of my head?" I swear, it was beginning to frustrate the hell out of me. The Rodeo was over a week ago, and I still couldn't get over how damn sexy she looked. I'd always enjoyed the Houston Rodeo. It was a good time for me to catch up with my boys from college. I looked forward to the BBQ contests and the livestock show, but my mind was preoccupied this year. It filled me with joy watching Naomi have a good time with Tess and her rowdy crew. But whenever I tried to get her alone or take her to check something out, Tess came. That wasn't even necessary; I wanted Naomi to experience everything.

A burst of air left my lips as I looked down, trying to refocus on my workout.

"Okay, what in the hell is wrong, dude?" Terrell asked with a laugh.

"What?"

"We've been in this gym for over twenty minutes. You would have started talking shit by now; what's up?"

"Nothing," I grunted, lifting my dumbbells.

"Uh-huh, so it's Ladybug again; you finally accepted that you've fallen for your sister?"

"Sister! What the hell are you talking about, Terrell?" I asked, confused and disgusted.

"Shit, I don't know what else to call it; you know our family dynamics are weird as fuck, but I'm all for it. I'm rooting for you and Ladybug. Please don't tell me you're trippin' about Nathan?"

"Naw, it's more than that. Tess told me to keep my distance until we've both healed. Hey, I wanted to ask a question?"

"What's up?"

"Do you think I'm still fucked up over that Brie shit?"

He stopped what he was doing to give me his undivided attention.

"I'm not going to lie, I was worried about you for a long time, but as time passed, I knew you would be alright. I was going to make sure of it. I love Nay, so you have my blessing with that whole brother-sister union." He laughed hard at his own joke.

"She's my sister's ex-husband's soon-to-be ex-wife; you know there's no blood ties."

"So, it's still weird ass fuck; now come on, let's knock this shit out and get out of here."

I laughed, jogging in place to get my blood pumping.

The next evening, I walked out of the hospital and sluggishly approached my truck.

"Are you sure you don't want to come over?" Katrina asked from behind.

"Naw, not tonight; that double shift wore me out. I know I

will be out when my head hits the pillow," I told her over my shoulder, not stopping.

"Why don't you let me give you something to ensure you sleep good." She suggestively licked her lips, glancing over to my truck.

Watching her lick those pretty lips reminded me how long it'd been.

Katrina was a cute nurse I had been hooking up with off and on since I started my residency.

"Naw, I'm good tonight." I slowed my stride to turn to her briefly. "Plus, I don't move like that near my place of work, and neither should you. We're better than that. Have a good night, and drive safely." I continued to my truck and climbed in. I rested my head back and rubbed my tired eyes. Of course, that was all some bullshit because if Naomi wanted to suck my di—. Nope, nope, nope. I cut that line of thinking off and started my truck. I pulled out of the parking garage, leaving a pissed Katrina in my wake.

Katrina wasn't the only woman I'd had to turn down recently. I kept a few regulars in rotation reaching out, wondering where I'd been. *What in the hell is wrong with me? The woman doesn't even belong to me, and she's changing me.* I'd worked hard to get where I am. I finally got past Brie's bullshit. Another woman hadn't crossed my mind as much as Brie until Naomi. And that scared the shit out of me.

I drove home tonight instead of crashing at Tess's. I needed time to think. Maybe Tess was right; I needed to keep my distance from Naomi.

CHAPTER NINETEEN

Naomi

"Tess, can you please tell me why in the world we are at a cake-decorating workshop?" Mona asked while whipping the butter creme in her bowl.

"Because Teddy got me the cutest pink-and-white apron with ruffles, I wanted to show him a more domesticated side of me. I plan to bake him a cake wearing nothing but that apron and a pair of pink high heel shoes to show him my appreciation. Plus, I figured this workshop would be a fun girls' night out."

"For you, maybe, but my big mama taught me how to cook a long time ago," Mona told her.

"Bitch, I can cook. I just don't know how to bake."

Mona looked at me and Robyn, thoroughly confused. "Is there a difference?"

We turned to Tess, laughing.

"Y'all shut the hell up; it will still be a fun girls' night."

"I've been meaning to ask you, Tess. What's up with all the pink?" Robyn asked, turning to look at her.

"I like pink. Pink is my signature color," she said with a Southern accent.

"Alright, Shelby, is this your 'Steel Magnolias' moment or something?"

"Well, Robyn, since you must know," Tess started sweetly, "just like ear hustling is your superpower, the color pink is mine, so mind your business."

"Rude," Robyn told her with a stink face, causing Tess to lick her tongue out at her, making her laugh.

"What kind of cake are you thinking of making for him?" I chimed in.

"Girl, the hell if I know; the plan is for him to eat *my* cake when it's time for dessert."

"Y'all so nasty," Robyn said, laughing.

"You have no idea. As you can see, I'm not a small woman, but the way that man can lift me like I weigh nothing and eat me…"

"We got it, Tess, damn. You don't have to rub it in our faces." Mona huffed with attitude.

"Don't be jealous, Mo Mo; I already told you I would teach you."

"I don't need to be taught a damn thing. Hell, I can teach a whole class on how to please a man," she mumbled under her breath, making me cackle.

"Mmmm, this is so good! Teddy is going to love this." Tess licked a piece of frosting from her finger, closing her eyes to savor the sweet buttery flavor. "We might need to make this a staple in the bedroom."

"How is it you and Teddy don't have a house full of kids?" Robyn asked, shaking her head.

"After we got married, the twins were still young. I figured we would take some time to enjoy each other, but lately, I can tell my big man is ready for a baby. I'm so glad you brought that up. So which one of you is going to get pregnant with me? It will be fun! Going to Lamaze together and getting maternity massages."

Silence.

"Yeah, Tess, I want no part of that," Robyn said, too focused on her cake now.

"You're going to need somebody to lean on for moral support once you're big; that can be me, but having a baby? No, can do, mama," Mona said.

"Naomi, come on, help a sister out."

"Do I look like the Virgin Mary to you, Tess, because the only way I'm getting pregnant is through immaculate conception?"

They all stopped what they were doing to look over at me as if to make sure that it came from me.

"Well, damn, Naomi," Mona said with pride.

"There she goes! I knew her quiet ass had it in her," Robyn replied loudly.

"Ladies, could you please lower your voices," the instructor said with annoyance, tired of our shit.

"Please forgive us; we will keep it down," Tess told her before turning to me with merriment in her eyes. "Touché bitch," she said with a wink.

Naomi

"Damn it! Not again!" I screamed, trying to avoid the cold spray of my now-ruined shower. I'd been having trouble with this damn shower for the past week. I was so happy Rob and Tee were coming over to fix it today. The thought of seeing their handsome faces almost made me forget about my ruined shower, *almost.*

I snatched my bath towel off the rack, stepped out of the

shower, and dried off. I paused when I picked up on the faint sound of my phone ringing in my bedroom. I hurried out to answer it. I tried to lunge across the bed for it but lost my balance and towel in the process.

"Hello," I huffed.

"Hey there, Ladybug, open up, we're at the door, and I hope you got some food to eat. Getting me up at this ungodly hour."

"Here I come, bye," I sang, ending the call. I stood there, butt naked, before I grabbed my purple kaftan my sister Zena bought me for a birthday one year. After putting it on, I glanced in the mirror to check my reflection. At times like these, I loved having short hair. I smiled as I rushed to attach my bracelets and put on a pair of hoop earrings. I applied some lip gloss and hurried to open the door.

When I opened it, I came face-to-face with a frowning Terrell.

"First off, rude for hanging up in my face like that, and you take your own sweet damn time answering the door. I swear Ladybug, our friendship is holding on by this much." He held his thick fingers up to demonstrate.

"Boy." I rolled my eyes and opened my arms as he pulled me in for a bear hug. After he put me down, I moved to the side to grant entry.

"Hey, Rob," I called out once Terrell was out of the way, allowing my gaze to sweep over the beautiful man standing in front of me.

"How's it going, Nay." He dropped a kiss on my cheek and walked past.

Damn, he smelled good.

"How are you liking it here so far?" Terrell asked, turning to look around my small 850-square-foot apartment. I was going for a Zen vibe with the shades of blue and green. I looked at a couple of other places but decided on this one. I was sold on the floor-to-ceiling window only this one had. It was my favorite place to stand and look out when I needed to ease my mind.

"I love it. It's close to everything, plus the art scene here in Houston is next level," I told him, smiling.

"Good, I knew you wouldn't have a hard time adjusting, hell if you could stay in a house with your husband's ex—. Ouch, Ladybug!" he shouted, rubbing his arm where I pinched him. "Now you're abusing me too; show me where the problem is so I can fix it and be on my way." He crossed his huge arms and pouted. I stood next to him and tried not to laugh.

"You are so silly," I told him.

"I swear, that's all you two do is clown around; where's the problem, Nay."

"Um, this way, it's the bathroom in my bedroom; follow me." Momentarily caught off guard by his tone, I turned and walked toward my room. When we reached my door, Terrell's phone began to ring.

"Y'all go ahead. I have to take this; it's a new client. I will be right back." He stepped back outside to answer his phone in private.

"Okay," I said.

As soon as we walked into my bedroom, my eyes scanned the towel and discarded clothes scattered on the floor. Feeling embarrassed, I mumbled excuse me, as I rushed over to grab everything off the floor and dropped it into the basket. When I looked back at Rob, I froze. I watched his hot gaze travel the length of my body.

Oh shit, I forgot, I didn't put anything on under this kaftan. I was pretty sure he could see *everything* when I bent over like that. I closed my eyes and groaned; I was beyond mortified. Shit.

I finally found the courage to open my eyes and took in the sexy smirk that had spread across his lips. He clearly was in a better mood.

"So right in there?" He pointed, still grinning as he walked toward the bathroom.

"Mhm," was all I could say with a tight smile.

"Okay, I'm going to get started," he said, walking passed, brushing against me. He paused to look down into my eyes before continuing into the bathroom.

Once he was inside and out of view, I flopped down onto the bed and brought the towel up to bury my face.

"Okay, what did I miss?" Terrell asked when he walked into the room.

~

Rob

She's trying to kill me. I'm convinced of it now.

She gotta be, bending over in front of me like that. That thin purple dress pulled tight over that luscious body damn near stopping my heart. I swear her body was calling my name. I might have done something stupid if she wasn't so embarrassed after realizing too late she was putting on a show for me that I loved. I had to stay away; the need to touch her was becoming unbearable. Terrell could have handled that faucet without me. I knew it would hurt, but it was the only way. My heart constricted at the thought of not seeing her perfect face.

CHAPTER TWENTY

Naomi

I couldn't help feeling that Rob had been distancing himself from me. When I asked Terrell about it, he would only say that everything was cool and that Rob had been busy working double shifts at the hospital.

"Yeah, okay, Tee," I said absently. "You would tell me if something was up, right?"

"Yes, for sure, Ladybug. When I talked to him this morning, he said he was off today and planned to stay home and catch up on his sleep."

"Okay, if you're sure everything's okay, I will see him in a few days. Tell him I said hey when you talk to him, and to call me, okay?"

"Will do, sis."

The "sis" surprised me, but I wasn't mad at it. I considered them family too. While sitting there, an idea formed in my mind. I got up from the couch and headed into my bedroom to get ready.

If the mountain won't come to Mohammed

~

An hour later, I put both bags in one hand to knock on the door.

"Who is it?" I heard the familiar deep voice ask.

"It's your fairy godmother; now open up," I replied, trying to shake off the nervousness.

All the way here, I kept debating if I should turn around and go back home. If the man didn't want to see me, I should respect his wishes. But he was my friend, and I missed him.

What if he had company? Female company? Well, it was too late now, I thought as the door began to open.

"Naomi." Surprise colored his face before I was rewarded with the most beautiful smile.

Relief swept through me. It gave me the courage to say what I needed to say.

"Someone mentioned to me that you've been working extra hard at the hospital taking care of the good people, so I figured the least I could do was drive out here to feed a friend." I lifted the bags of Chinese food.

What he did next caught me by surprise. He pulled me inside and placed the bags I was carrying on the table and pulled me into his arms.

"Thank you, Nay. This was a wonderful surprise," he said, still holding me close.

"No problem, Rob," I hugged him back, happy he was as glad to see me as I was him.

Once inside, I walked over to place my things on the table and paused. "Um, Rob, what's that I'm smelling?" I asked, picking up on a familiar scent. I turned to look into his bashful stare.

He released a nervous chuckle before he cleared his throat. "You picked up on that, did you?"

"Yeah, I did," I told him with a smile.

"In my defense, a while back, when I went to grab some of my things out of Tess's spare bedroom, the smell was the first thing I noticed walking in. The scent was amazing. To my surprise, the candle was on the dresser. I may have brought it with me on my way out."

"So you like my smell, huh?" I asked him with a smile.

"You have no idea." He tilted his head, biting his lower lip.

Okay, he won. I couldn't play with him as Tee, and I played around. Tee's response would have been, *"Sure if you're going for that old lady mothball scent, but hey, do you."* I thought with a chuckle.

"Well … I will grab one for you the next time I go shopping. Now come on, let's eat."

"So, this is the infamous bachelor pad, huh?" I paused to look around as we ate.

"Who told you that?" he asked with a laugh.

"Terrell," I told him in a matter-of-fact tone.

At the mention of his best friend, he laughed harder.

"He had to be messing with you. He knows no woman besides Tess, and now you have stepped foot in here. I've always gone back to their—" he stopped mid-sentence as embarrassment covered his handsome face.

I dropped my fork, threw my head back, and laughed. Once the words came out full steam, he had to go with it.

"You should have seen your face." I pointed at him as I got to my feet. I glanced around before asking, "Bathroom?"

"Sure, it's the last door on your left."

I continued to giggle as I walked away.

Over the next few hours, we watched a movie, laughed, and enjoyed each other's company. By the end of the film, I had my legs curled under me and was laying my head on his chest. Neither one of us moved.

"Naomi, there's something I want to tell you," he said gruffly.

"What's up?" I asked, turning my head to gaze up as my cell started ringing. I looked down to see Nathan's number. At any other time, I wouldn't have answered, but Livy was with him.

"Uh, it's Nathan; he has Livy. I have to take this."

"No worries, you can go into the spare bedroom next to the bathroom for some privacy."

"Thank you."

After I went inside, I hit talk. "Yes, Nathan, is everything alright?"

"Where are you, Naomi?" he demanded.

I didn't respond right away. I would not show my ass in front of Rob.

Once I could answer without yelling, I told him, "I'm visiting a friend, is everything alright?"

"You don't have any friends, Naomi, so where are you?"

Ignoring him, I calmly said, "I'm going to assume Livy is fine because if she weren't, I know that would have been the first thing you would have stated. So if there isn't anything else, Nathan, I will see you tomorrow when you drop Livy off."

"Yes, you will." He disconnected the call.

I refused to allow Nathan to ruin this fun evening. After I got my mind together, I put a smile on my face and went back out to join Rob.

"Is everything okay? he asked, cleaning off the table.

"Yes, just Nathan being Nathan," I told him as I played with my bracelets.

He walked over and sat on the arm of his black leather sofa.

"Those are gorgeous bracelets. I know I've told you that already. Do you mind if I have a closer look?" he asked as he held out his hands and widened his long legs so I could come in close.

"Ah, sure." I walked over to him on autopilot, holding my wrists out.

"So, what was the occasion?" he asked while inspecting one then the other.

"Excuse me?"

"You mentioned you bought these for yourself at the twins' birthday party. Was there a special occasion?"

"Ah yeah, you could say that. I had recently completed a difficult training; I felt a celebration was in order."

We talked as he cradled my hands, rubbing his thumbs over the bracelets and continued his inspection.

In all the years Nathan and I had been together, he never asked to see my bracelets, to look this closely. I tried to remain calm, but it shook me.

My stomach lurched when his fingers glided along the underside of my wrists, slightly nudging my bracelets up. I immediately snatched my hands away in shock.

"What in the hell do you think you're doing, Rob?" I asked, staring into his knowing eyes.

"I don't know, Naomi," was his weary reply as he continued to watch me. "Listen, whenever you're ready to talk about it, I'm here."

How did he figure it out?

"I don't know what you're talking about or what you think you may know," I told him, feeling completely exposed. "Look, this was fun," I said, walking over to gather my things. "But I need to get going."

"Naomi, wait, I'm sorry I didn't mean to push; I just care so much about you and want you to know I'm here. You can talk to me about anything." His eyes tracked my movements.

I paused to look over to see he hadn't left his spot. He sat there, watching me, with his hand over his heart.

I dropped my head, trying to block out the concern shimmering in his eyes. "I'll see you later, Rob." I slipped out the door and damn near ran to my car.

I threw everything on the passenger seat as I climbed inside and shut my door. I closed my eyes while breathing deeply, trying to get my emotions under control.

Well, shit.

CHAPTER TWENTY-ONE

Nathan

She didn't think I knew where she was. She went to see Tess's brother. It was one thing if she couldn't seem to look past my slip-up, but it was another thing to embarrass me like this in front of Tess and those gladiator rejects. I hoped she would have come back home once she realized I wasn't paying for an apartment. She hadn't worked since we lived in Texas! Who would have thought she could have acclimated enough to pay for a whole apartment? I tried to give her space to teach her a lesson. I figured she would come running back to me. It would have worked if she hadn't teamed up with Medusa. *How is it even possible for a woman to ruin your life twice?* Tess had already taken one family from me; now she was trying to take my new one! I bet Teddy's finding this funny, laughing at how pathetic I am.

Did Naomi not realize how bad this made me look in my client's eyes? Did she even care?

I never would have imagined she would be out there thriving without me or my money. She made a big mistake getting close to Tess and her family. She and Livy belong to me!

I'm looking like a fool over here while Teddy is with my ex-wife and children. Now he wanted my current wife and child too! No. I had to help Naomi from making this mistake. With an idea firmly in place, I grabbed my phone and hesitated. *I needed someone to help Naomi see the mistake she was making.*

～

Naomi

Today, Tess and I planned to do some shopping. When I arrived at her house, she was finishing up with her client in her office. I went into the kitchen to get something to drink and waited.

"Hey Naomi," she called, poking her head out of her office.

I scooted my chair back and walked toward her office.

"Can you grab those green folders off the counter in my bathroom?" she asked.

"Sure," I said, happy I was here to help; she didn't like to leave her clients alone in her office.

Normally, I steered clear of people's personal space, but there wasn't much I wouldn't do for Tess, and the heifer knew that.

Once I entered the grand bathroom, I stopped as a loud gasp left my lips. *I knew it; I knew I should have just stayed my ass out of there.* I chastised myself as I took in the sight before me. Behind the beautiful bathtub in the middle of the large suite was a larger-than-life portrait, almost the size of the wall. It was the back of a naked Teddy in all his glory. The picture was *stunning.* He stood in a gladiator pose that showcased every well-defined muscle underneath his glistening deep-chocolate skin. The only thing missing was a sword and a shield. I'd seen Teddy in his gym close many times, but the portrait showed how magnificent his physique was. I saw Teddy as my brother, so I hurried and looked away. He had a nice ass, but no one wanted to see their brother's naked ass. "Ew." I found the folders she wanted and damn near ran from the room.

As I walked back downstairs, her clients were leaving out the front door. She looked up and waited for me at the bottom.

"You know you ain't right, don't you?" I asked, handing her the folders.

"What?" she asked with all innocence.

"You know why, and have Mona and Robyn seen that?" I whispered.

"Yep, that's why they're so jelly," she said with a wink, walking back into her office.

"It doesn't make you feel some type of way about other women seeing him?" I asked, following behind her. "Let me tell you, if it were me, I would never allow another woman inside that room," I told her, pointing upstairs. "I would tackle somebody down to the ground before they stepped across the threshold."

She howled with laughter. "Girl, that picture was from a photo shoot he did years ago. I'm sure it can still be found online somewhere. Teddy will demand attention whether he's wearing clothes or not; my baby is spectacular. To look at him, you would swear he's a heartbreaker up and down, but that couldn't be further from the truth. All that nonsense went to Terrell, thank god. Teddy is one of the most consistent men I've ever met. Even when we were teenagers. I wasn't shocked when he joined the military; it suited him. Anyway, to answer your question, it doesn't make me feel anything other than gratitude knowing all that man is mine."

"Okay, but are there any other rooms I should be made aware of?" I asked with all seriousness. All the crazy woman did was laugh.

CHAPTER TWENTY-TWO

Tonight is the night.

Naomi

"Mommy, somebody is calling on your phone!"

"Thank you, baby. Are those banana waffles good?" I asked, grabbing my cell off the counter and scrolling through my text messages.

"They're delicious!" she shouted with a huge grin.

"That's what I like to hear."

I'd received several calls and texts from Rob over the past few days. The last text put a smile on my face. I was not upset with him; I was embarrassed by how I ran out of there, like a scared little girl. I knew I could trust him; I was looking forward to talking to him about my past. To be completely open, no hiding. Something I'd become quite good at. I opened his message to shoot him a text.

Me: Hey you, Dinner at my place around eight?

Rob: Sounds good, Ladybug!

"Oh, hell no," I chuckled.

Me: Uh, please don't start; I'm trying to break Tee from that Ladybug crap.

Rob: LOL, I think it's cute.

Rob: What do you need me to bring?

Me: Just you; I got it covered.

"Did you hear me, mommy?"

"I'm sorry, baby; what did you say?" I asked, giving my daughter my undivided attention.

"I said I'm going to make banana waffles for Nya and Nate Jr. tomorrow morning."

"Well, I know they are going to love them," I told her with a smile.

She would shout excitedly whenever she mentioned her siblings, making me chuckle.

"Finish up, baby girl; Uncle Tee and the kids will be here to pick you up soon, so we have to hurry.

"Okay, mommy."

Later that evening, while straightening up, a huge grin slit my face when I heard the doorbell.

I glanced at the clock on the wall to see it was only 6:45 p.m.

That's odd; Rob said he wouldn't be here until eight p.m.

It could only be Tess or Terrell; those two were notorious for popping up.

When I opened the door, my smile immediately fell.

"Mom, Dad, what are you doing here?" I asked, looking into my parent's stern faces.

"We received a disturbing call from Nathan. Apparently, you've gotten yourself into some trouble; we need to talk Naomi."

I released a hard sigh before stepping to the side to let them in.

An hour later

"Why, Naomi, can't you be more like your siblings? They have never given us an ounce of trouble. They're both excelling in their lives and careers. What would cause a smart, beautiful young woman to lose her mind and start making crazy and impulsive decisions? You quit your job and cut off all of your beautiful hair?"

"I've told you both multiple times when I decided to live a healthier lifestyle; the first thing that had to go was my chemically relaxed hair. I no longer desired to have long, straight hair down my back. It's been over seven years now, and I can tell you both that it was still one of the best decisions I could have ever made. My big chop started me on a healthier path to a more balanced lifestyle. I guess you both were blind to the fact that it was killing me, trying always to be perfect."

My mother continued as if I hadn't said a word.

"Then, you go on to do something stupid like befriending your husband's ex-wife! Are you that desperate for friends, Naomi? That you would throw your dignity right out the window? Get you and Livy's things. You can't make it on your own." Disgust coated her words as the frown on her mocha-brown face deepened.

I was trying my damnedest to reign in my temper. "Maybe it's because you have a daughter that's suffered from mental illness for most of her life that you both didn't want to acknowledge. You see weakness, but I can assure you I'm far from weak. You can't even recognize all the work I've put in; you only see a daughter who tried to off herself when life got too hard. I suffered in silence for so long. In the beginning, I was too young to understand why all my friends and siblings were always happy, and I often had to pretend to be happy. I tried coming to you, and you both said it was normal to get down. I don't fault you for not knowing the signs of clinical depression, but at least you could have acknowledged you had a child that suffered from mental illness."

"I'm sorry, I just don't get it," my mother began, shaking her head, "if someone can't appreciate the gift of life by attempting to take their own life, I don't think they are fit to be in society."

"Wow, it's that black and white mom? You don't think I'm fit to be in society?"

Her silence sliced through me. Sadness gripped my heart, causing me to stagger. It was nothing I hadn't heard before, but it still hurt. I worked so hard to have a better life, to live life, not to only exist in it. They didn't see any of it.

"All that money on education went down the drain," my father started.

I took a shaky breath to control my hurt. "Why can't you both understand I don't need saving? I'm good. My life here is good. Nathan is the one that messed this up, not me. He's the one that was caught with another woman in our bed. I bet he didn't mention that little bit, did he? I'm trying to make the best of a difficult situation. So if you want to be mad at somebody, be mad at him because I've done nothing wrong. But unfortunately, both of you are unable to see that. Your basket-case daughter is coming unhinged again, right?" I said with a humorless laugh trying not to cry.

They glanced at one another, remaining silent as if agreeing with my statement that clearly dripped with sarcasm.

Unbelievable.

"Come on, Naomi, what kind of woman has dealings with her husband's ex-wife? Only a fool would do such a thing." My mother said shaking her head.

Of course, I wouldn't expect my parents to understand. They'd always seen me as broken. Unbalanced. Tess could give a damn what anybody thought. I was quickly adopting that mindset.

"And that poor little girl. She has to be front row to all of this. You need to pack your things and come home with us, Naomi. I knew at some point this would happen, and we would have to bail you out of something. Let's get ahead of this before any rumors start. We do have *our* reputation to think about, Naomi Olivia. Did you ever stop to think about how this would affect us?" My mother finished.

As I listened to them tear into me, I lowered my chin to my chest, closed my eyes, and tried to focus on my breaths.

"Okay, that's enough. I'm sorry, Nay, if you're not going to say something, I for damn sure will."

Hearing Rob's deep voice, my eyes flew open as he walked inside.

"Look, I showed up ten minutes ago. I heard you in here talking and didn't want to interrupt, but that's it. The attack on Naomi stops now; I don't give a damn who the hell you both are. Did you come all this way to ambush your own child?" he asked in disbelief.

"Does this man defending you know how unstable you are, Naomi? That you were committed to a mental institution? And what you tried to do that led you there?" my mother asked, looking at me.

"Young man, you sound like you care for my daughter, but if she didn't tell you, she's a married woman with a child," my father informed him.

"And that poor little girl." My mother sniffled behind him.

They were expecting Rob to hightail it out of there, but he caught everyone by surprise when he started to laugh.

"Wow," he said, clapping his hands. "I wish I had an award

for 'Best Performance' to give you both. That was amazing; so passionate. Wasn't it?" he asked, looking over at me.

"Excuse me?" my father asked, shock written all over his face.

"Your performance was amazing, top tier," Rob repeated, smiling with his arms crossed.

"Son, nothing was remotely funny about what was said, and surely not a performance. That's my daughter; I know her."

"Sir, I must stop you right there. That may be your daughter, but judging by what the two of you just said, you don't know anything about Naomi. I can't speak on California Naomi, but let me tell you a little about Texas Naomi. I've seen a woman thrive. She puts the needs of her daughter above her own. She takes excellent care of herself and everyone around her. She's smart, ambitious, and has overcome a huge obstacle that more than fifty-seven million Americans face. So instead of trying to shame her, maybe you should applaud and celebrate the strength and courage she has shown. You know, like loving caring parents would do."

"Naomi! I know you won't just stand there and allow this man to insult us like this," my father demanded.

"Dad, to answer your questions, I'm not going back to Nathan, and no, I'm not moving back to California. You and Mom can leave if that's all you came here for. I love you both, but I'm tired of allowing you to make me feel this way."

My parents marched out the front door.

Once they were gone, Rob wrapped his arms around me. I tried to pull away a couple of times, mumbling that I was fine, but each time he held me tighter. I gave up and rested my head on his chest, and let the tears fall from my eyes. After several minutes he led me over to the couch to sit down.

"Rob, I would like to share something with you."

He shook his head to stop me. "You don't have to explain

anything to me or feel obligated to share something you're not ready for, Naomi." He looked into my eyes.

"I know I don't, and I appreciate you saying that. I planned on talking to you about everything tonight anyway."

"Okay, talk to me, Nay," he said, giving me his undivided attention.

I took a cleansing breath. "I'm just going to dive right in. I know you already have an idea what's under these bracelets." I lifted them.

"I do," he replied softly, grabbing one of my hands and giving it an encouraging squeeze.

"I'm not sure how you knew, but you seemed to have figured it out. After all the years wearing my bracelets, I've never met anyone with an inkling of what I was hiding underneath them. Other than the occasional comment on how expensive they are, nothing. I have to ask, what made you notice?"

He cleared his throat. "The only way I can answer that is to simply say I know you, Naomi. I made it a point to know everything about you. From the way you walk, the way you talk, down to the slope of that gorgeous hook on the back of your head." He paused to laugh; I rolled my eyes with a smile.

He leaned close. "How you cared for yourself intrigued me. How meticulous you were. I've also noticed no matter what you're going through, you find the time to always put yourself first in some capacity. Walking, painting, meditating, you find something to ground yourself, even while dealing with Nathan and Livy's accident. Those were traumatic times for you, but you didn't falter. I know firsthand how trauma can bring you to your knees," he hesitated, "and make you question if you could continue to go on with all the pain inside."

I studied the haunted look that crossed his handsome face. I had an idea what he was thinking about, but I wouldn't bring up Brie until he was ready to talk about it. It was my time to share my demons.

"You absently touch those bracelets in stressful situations; I could tell they soothed you in some way. I finally put two and two together and wanted to check. I'm sorry about that. No one should force you to share something like that until you're ready."

"I appreciate that, Rob. There's only been a couple of people I've felt comfortable enough sharing something so personal with until you and Tess. I've learned that depression is a thief, a killer of joy and happiness, and if left untreated, it can be deadly. I almost found that out the hard way." I looked down at my bracelets.

"From that dark place I was in, if you had told me it would get better, I would have called you a liar. I remember the first time Dr. Tracy came to see me. She told me the depression I felt was an illness; like any illness, it needed a treatment plan. The place I was in mentally at the time, I didn't think there was hope for me." I paused when his large warm hand closed around mine, giving it a gentle squeeze.

I sandwiched his hand between mine, appreciating the warm gesture.

"I remember Dr. Tracy told me I had such a bright future. Her plea was simple: 'Please, Naomi, please trust me enough to help you; I promise it will get better.' So I did; I let her help me. And as time went on, each day got a tiny bit brighter, not by much, but enough to give me a little hope, which I desperately needed at the time. So with the help of therapy and medication, the black cloud over me began to pass. It was never gone completely, but far enough to breathe again. To smile again, to laugh again. Slowly I began to see myself less as a victim and more as a survivor because I survived! I refused to allow depression to deal me a death sentence. I learned how to identify my triggers and how to manage my stress. I listened to my body and gave it what it needed. I know I will have to do this for the rest of my life, but it's a battle I will win. I have a wonderful life, despite what's happened recently. I will not allow anyone to take that from me because I know where that could lead.

"Sadly, my family sees things differently. And that's alright. I wish they could understand that mental illness is real, but not my problem to try and convince them. I know who I am and how strong I am." I looked into his eyes with a smile.

I didn't see pity swimming in his warm brown eyes. What I saw made my smile grow.

He released a heavy exhale. "I mean this from the bottom of my heart when I say this. You're superwoman in my eyes, Naomi. A black, sexy-as-hell superwoman and you got me all snared in your golden lasso."

"What?" I said, releasing a crack of laughter.

"I don't know what I'm even saying; you see how you got me?"

We were quiet, looking deep into each other's eyes.

"I've never met anyone stronger than you, man or woman. Nay. Stay here; I'll be right back," he said after getting to his feet and disappearing into my bedroom.

I sat back and folded my legs under me. I couldn't believe my parents came all this way to do what they had done my entire life. They didn't ask about Livy or how I was doing. They didn't even hug or tell me it was good to see me. But of course, they let me know how my actions could affect their reputation. Wow.

I was deep in thought and barely caught what Rob was saying.

"Excuse me?" I asked, looking up at him.

He stood in front of me with his hands out.

"I said to come with me. I ran you a bath, and don't worry about cooking; I will run out to pick something up. We're going to restart the evening, okay? Only good thoughts." He smiled, grabbing my hands and pulling me to my feet.

"Only good thoughts," I echoed, doing my best not to think about my parents any longer.

~

I jumped when someone tapped on the bathroom door.

"It's me, Naomi. Are you still in the bath?" Rob's deep voice asked through the door.

"Um yeah," I told him as I sat up.

"Okay, I wanted to let you know I was back. I hope you don't mind," he hesitated, "I put something on your bed for you to put on. Come out when you're ready."

"Thanks, Rob; I will be right out," I told him, standing from the tub, trying not to laugh at the sweet gesture.

Let me go and see what the man has picked out.

I walked over to my bed and looked at my choices. On the left, a pair of boy shorts and a tank top; the other option was only my fluffy white bathrobe. *What the hell,* I bit my lower lip and looked toward the door with a frown.

As if reading my mind, he laughed.

"You're probably in there thinking, what kind of freaky shit is this man trying to get into. I can assure you; it's nothing like that." More serious, he said, "Look, Naomi, that was pretty shitty what your parents were saying. And that was only from the little I caught as I was walking up. I want to ease your mind and help you relax."

"Okay…" I said, not knowing where he was going with this.

"I'm pretty sure my sister has already told you everything about me, but in case she hasn't, I used to be a massage therapist while in college. Not those freaky massages; my clients typically were patients that recently had surgeries requiring massages to aid healing. I want to give you a massage if you don't mind?"

"First off, your sister never mentioned you being a whole massage therapist out here, and second, give me two seconds; I will be right out."

"Great, get changed, I'm going to finish setting up out here, and Naomi, please wear whichever you think you'll feel most comfortable."

I turned back to look down at my options again. It only took me a second to decide as I bit my lip with a huge smile. I grabbed what I felt most comfortable with, changed, and walked out.

"Wow," I whispered breathlessly, walking into my living room. In that short time, Rob had transformed the space into a mini day spa.

He looked my way when he heard me approach, offering a warm smile.

"Everything is so beautiful, Rob." I looked around at the candles that softly lit the room. The smell of jasmine and vanilla wafted through the air. Anita Baker played in the background. *How did he know that I loved Anita Baker?*

My eyes landed on the massage table and the lotions and oils on the side table.

"You really thought of everything, but I have to ask, do you randomly ride around with a mini massage parlor in your truck?" I asked playfully, curious to hear his answer.

"That does seem kinda strange, doesn't it?" he said with a chuckle.

"Maybe just a little bit," I told him, showing my fingers to measure.

"To be honest, Naomi, I've been planning to give you a massage for a long time now; I've been waiting for the right moment. I wanted to be prepared *when* the time came."

"When?"

"You caught that, did you? I figured if I stayed ready, I wouldn't have to get ready; you feel me?" He smiled, biting his lip, watching me.

"Whatever, and why Anita Baker?" I asked suspiciously.

"I told you, I made it my business to learn all your likes and dislikes," he said over his shoulder while he finished setting up.

"Oh really," I challenged.

"Yep, try me?"

Okay, Mr. Know It All, I will start with an easy one; what's my favorite movie?"

"*The Notebook.*"

"My favorite color?"

"Easy, purple. That's one of the first things I noticed about you. I loved the different shades of purple you wear."

"Okay, what's my favorite scent?"

"Vanilla, cocoa butter, and Japanese cherry blossom. They have become my favorite scents as well," he said, licking his lips, causing my sex to clinch.

"Okay, food?"

"Come on, Naomi, give me some credit. You're going to have to ask something a little more difficult."

"Alright, what is my pet peeve?"

"When rude people interrupt, not allowing the other person to speak freely."

I stood there looking into his smiling face with my mouth open. Recovering, I cleared my throat and said, "Um, a weakness?"

"Sometimes, not seeing how strong you are," he said with a seriousness that made me want to look away.

"And strength?"

"That's a hard one." He rubbed his hands together.

"You have so many, but I'm going to have to say, knowing your self-worth, which is something I know you're going to pass on to your beautiful little girl."

"Pretty good, Rob. I'm impressed," I told him with a big smile.

"I don't know everything ... yet, but give me time. We're just getting started. So if the lady is ready, please place your robe on the chair."

He probably assumed I had on the boy shorts and tank top

he laid out, but he would soon see I went with the second option. I thought nervously.

Damn, it seemed like a good idea in the room; now I was second-guessing my stupid plan.

"Nay, are you ready?"

I waited for a second longer then said *fuck it.* Opening the robe, I shrugged it off my shoulders. I did not miss the quick air intake. I placed the robe on the sofa and walked toward the table.

"Where do you want me?"

"Excuse me?"

I couldn't help smiling. "How do you want me on the table?" I gestured toward it.

"Let's start with you laying on your stomach," he said, snapping out of his daze.

"Okay."

I walked to one side and did as he asked. Once on my stomach, he draped a folded sheet across my butt. A bottle cap snapped open before the delicious scent of almond oil and lavender filled the air. I rested my head on the face cradle, trying to relax.

I jumped when I felt his strong hands on my shoulder.

"Easy Nay, this is all for you," he said soothingly.

His fingers ran along my shoulder blade to the base of my skull, where he took his time. I could feel his strong thumbs and fingers melting my tension away.

He continued to slide his warm hands down my back. I tried hard to keep my mind on the amazing massage instead of the fact that the front of him was inches away from my face. With him so close to my nude body, I couldn't stop my mind from wandering to the time I felt his big …

"How does that feel?"

"Hmm?"

"Is the pressure okay for you?"

"Yes, it's perfect." I breathed a long sigh.

I could have sworn I heard a soft chuckle.

Bastard.

Fifteen minutes into the massage, with his exceptional hands rubbing on my body, the sultry music in my ears and the heady aroma in the air, it was all starting to have an effect on my lady parts. I released an involuntary shudder when his hands absently skimmed the sides of my breasts as they rubbed down to my waist. His large hands covered my entire back as he continued to run them from my shoulders down to my spine. He repeated this movement with firm hands as he slipped them under the sheet to massage the top of my ass.

Keep it together, Naomi; it felt so damn good.

"How are you doing, beautiful?"

"So good," I told him, feeling his strong fingers kneading my ass, releasing tension from the muscle but slowly building another kind of tension.

He paused to walk to my feet at the opposite end of the table. His hands momentarily off my body gave me a chance to regroup. *I've got this; I've had massages in the past. Let me stop acting like I've never been touched by a man. Stop being pathetic, Naomi.* I would have laughed, but I felt him at my feet. He widened my legs slightly apart to access each leg better.

Oh hell.

I was in trouble when his hands wrapped around my calf and began to knead and work his thumbs deep into the muscle. He continued higher, working his thumbs into the back of my thigh.

Higher still, those wicked hands glided.

"Is this, okay?"

"Yes," I replied with a half moan.

"Good, if I do anything you don't like, just tell me to stop."

"I can assure you, that's one word that will not leave my lips."

He chuckled and got back to work.

I felt his hands run up along my inner thigh. I released a pent-up sigh as my thighs widened a bit on their own accord. I felt him still for a split second before he continued. I held my breath, anticipating his touch along the back of my pussy. He was so close. When I believed I would feel his fingers any second, he adjusted his stance to begin massaging the other calf, starting the whole process on the other leg. By the time he reached the top of my thigh, I was practically panting. His long skillful fingers slid along my slit this time, making me shudder.

"Can you turn over for me so I can do the front?" he whispered into my ear.

I was so relaxed and turned on I felt tipsy. I wasn't sure I could do it without falling off the table. He discreetly held the sheet up for me to turn over. But before he could drape it over me, our eyes connected.

"That was amazing, but …" I paused breathlessly.

He didn't say a word; he just continued to look down into my eyes.

"What do you need from me, Naomi?"

"You, right now," I told him without hesitation.

The music changed to Tank's "When We," causing the temperature in the already sexually charged room to spike.

"Are you sure this is what you want?" he asked, watching me closely.

I bit my lip, watching him as he tossed the sheet to the side. With eyes still on me, he slowly removed his shirt.

My eyes drank him in, *Lord, help me.*

"I'm waiting for your answer, gorgeous. Are you sure this is what you want?"

"Please fuck me Rob, right now. Is that answer enough for you?"

He strolled over to me before hefting me up from the table. I wrapped my legs around his waist as I sought his mouth. Once our tongues connected, my body went up in flames. My need for him consumed me. I began to whimper as I rubbed my drenched sex against his thickening erection as we tried to devour each other.

He held me close as he walked us into my bedroom and sat me on the bed before pulling down his pants.

When he stood back up, my mouth fell open. I was mesmerized as I watched his *huge* dick hit his stomach with a thud.

I'd felt it in my hand and knew it was big, but seeing it *hard* was *different.*

"Come on now, don't act like you didn't know," he said with a devilish grin, giving that monster a few slow strokes. "Don't worry; I promise you will be good and ready for me. Listen, Naomi, I want you to know this is more than just sex for me. Do you hear me?" The playful expression was gone from his handsome face.

"Yes," I answered, feeling the same way.

"I want to make you feel things."

He walked to my bed and climbed onto it. When he settled, he reached for me, dragging me across the bed to him before lifting me to straddle his large body. Once I was seated, he lay back, placed his hands behind his head, and watched me.

"Do you know how beautiful you are, Naomi?"

My nipples hardened under his lustful gaze.

I smiled, leaning forward to place a kiss on his soft lips.

"Do your thing, girl." His deep voice vibrated against my lips as I continued to kiss his neck. I shuddered when he slipped his hands down my spine to cup my ass, pushing down while he ground his dick into my pussy. I placed my hands on his chest as I sat up, slowly grinding on him and looking into his eyes.

"That's it, baby, get that pussy ready for me. You're so damn sexy. Looking like a beautiful goddess sitting on her throne." He reached up to palm my heavy breast. With his thickness nestled between my slick folds, I slid my drenched pussy back and forth along his length as my pleasure continued to build. I leaned forward to apply pressure to my engorged clit and moaned loudly.

"Are you ready for me?"

"Yes," I moaned, ready to burst.

"Good, brace yourself; it's about to get rough."

He lifted me by my waist and brought me down. Slowly. He stretched me wide to accommodate his large girth. It was good I was already soaking wet and relaxed; his entry could have been painful due to his sheer size. He filled me completely.

"You alright, baby?" he asked once I was fully seated as his hands ran all over my body. I quivered as goosebumps spread across my skin. Being this connected and feeling his touch everywhere, I began to experience sensory overload and started to squirm.

His large hands clamped down on my thighs, preventing any movement.

"Don't move; just feel it," he gritted out.

We were connected so intimately, staring into each other's eyes. My vaginal walls were desperately contracting against him, trying to draw him in deeper while simultaneously trying to expel him from so deep inside my body.

Oh god, the pressure.

"Rob, I … it's—" I panted as I searched his face with wide frantic eyes, my heart pounding.

"Don't worry; I've got you. Now, let me have it," he whispered.

He slid his thumb against my clit, adding the slightest pressure causing me to detonate. The feeling was so intense I threw my head back and released a soundless scream as my body shook from the sheer force of my release.

"That's it, Nay, give it all to me," he grunted harshly as my orgasm began to peak. Only then did he finally start to move inside me. His strong arms brought me to the tip before slamming me back down. He did this as if I weighed nothing. I was shaking as I placed my hands on his chest and started to ride his ass like a jockey in the Kentucky Derby.

"Ride that dick, baby, yeah, just like that," he gritted out, bringing me down harder with his hands at my waist.

Nothing was graceful about it; I wanted everything he had to give.

Our bodies were slick with sweat as our heavy breathing echoed around the room. I ignored the tingling in my thighs, not ready for the feeling to end.

I let out a small yelp when he sat up suddenly, wrapping his arms around me and holding on tightly. He dipped his head latching onto my nipple, drawing it deep into his mouth as he stroked inside me. He pulled on my nipple so hard I grunted loudly as my womb contracted. He released one nipple with a pop before attacking the other with the same fervor. It was all so overwhelming my movements faltered.

Uh-uh," he said, releasing my nipple. "Don't you stop riding my dick; you feel too damn good." He grabbed the back of my head, pulling me to him for a deep kiss. He sucked my bottom lip into his mouth before plunging his tongue deep inside, exploring every corner. I moaned into his kiss as he held my head in place and skillfully made love to my mouth with his tongue.

My god, the man was everywhere. Thrusting inside my body; his masculine scent filled my lungs as his taste lingered on my lips. His lovemaking was so potent I had to remember there was only one man who was making me feel all these things.

"I'm about to cum, baby; you ready for me?" he asked against my swollen lips.

"Yes!" I almost sobbed.

He placed a featherlight kiss on my parted quivering lips before his large body stilled. He tucked his head into my neck, groaning loudly as he began to pulse deep inside me, painting my walls in his essence. His release triggered my orgasm. It was almost painful in its intensity. I held on tightly, rolling my pelvis into his as it continued to wash over me.

After a moment, he rested his forehead against mine.

"Damn," he finally said, breathing hard.

"Damn," I echoed, trying to catch my breath. Because what else was there to say after experiencing something like that?

I kissed his lips and pulled him close to cradle his head against my slick breasts. I didn't know what was going through his head, but I wished we could have stayed like that forever, but sadly, I knew that wasn't possible.

CHAPTER TWENTY-THREE

Naomi

"Why aren't you asleep, baby?"

I looked over my shoulder to see Rob coming out of the bedroom, wearing only boxers. A smile spread across my lips as he walked toward me.

"Hey, how'd you sleep?"

"I was sleeping good until I reached over to find you gone. Everything okay?" he asked, coming in close and pulling me back against his warm chest. Feeling safe and protected, I nestled into his embrace as we stared into the still night.

I came out of the room twenty minutes ago to look out the window and reflect on everything that happened that evening. I loved every second of Rob's lovemaking, but now I felt conflicted. I'd also come to a few realizations. The first one was not a shocker; I was in love with Robert Mason. The man was so damn easy to love. But that did complicate things.

I still had to deal with Nathan, and Rob hadn't completely dealt with the hurt Brie caused. He believed he had, but I knew trauma too well. I'd suggest he talk to someone; it didn't have to be Dr. Tracy; even though she was amazing and helped me tremendously. He had to find someone he was comfortable with. I knew the consequence of suppressing trauma. I loved him too much to see him carrying that around. And lastly, Tess. That woman had come to mean the world to me in this short time. She was like the big sister I never had but always wanted. I wouldn't jeopardize that relationship for anything. So as much as I knew it would hurt, Rob and I couldn't do that. *Not now anyway,* I noted sadly.

"Rob, can I ask you a question?"

"Sure, what's up?" he smoothly asked.

I took a moment to ensure I was sensitive in my approach; I wanted him to be open and free to answer how he wanted.

"You know I'm big on wellness and mental health. I've noticed you are as well. You're in excellent shape. You eat healthy." I paused to breathe and dove right in. "Have you ever considered going to therapy after your breakup with Brie?" *There, I said it, prayed I didn't offend, and hoped he would answer.*

Surprisingly, he only took a minute before admitting that he had.

"To tell you the truth, I just didn't have the time for it. I threw myself into my work and worked extra hard in the gym. The funny thing is I believed I was dealing with it," he said with an empty laugh.

"That was until everything broke, and I ended up at my sister's house feeling like my world was on fire and I was suffocating. I stayed with Tess and Teddy for a while after that. During that time, I couldn't get Terrell to leave my side. I never saw that kind of worry in my brother's eyes, and we've done some pretty crazy and scary shit when we were young.

"But I got through it. I've dated women here and there. I never imagined I would ever meet another woman I was willing to risk opening up to again until you, Naomi. Getting to know you has shown me how much Brie took from me. Maybe it was my fault for thinking she was so perfect. I couldn't see the other side of her, like Tess and Terrell. All I know is I'm done being afraid.

"You deserve all of me, not half of a man that can't forgive what his ex did. No, I forgive her for what she did. I don't understand why she did it, but I still forgive her because I want to give the woman of my dreams everything I have to offer."

When he finished, silent tears ran down my face.

"I'm not trying to scare you, baby. I know you have a lot going on. Let's take this a day at a time. Does that work?"

I couldn't speak at the moment, so I nodded.

"Good, come on, let's go back to bed."

He kissed my neck and grabbed my hand, leading me back to the bedroom.

I listened to his soft snores and processed what he'd shared. Without a doubt, I loved this man, but the last thing I wanted to do was cause him any more pain. I had way too much going on right now. *What if it doesn't work out, and I end up hurting him?* I knew how hard it was for Tess to see her brother in that state. What about Teddy and Terrell? They could get hurt in all this as well. I released a heavy sigh after coming to the sad conclusion.

I couldn't do it. I couldn't risk hurting people that meant the world to me.

CHAPTER TWENTY-FOUR

Two weeks later

Naomi

"I hate this." I blew out. I snatched my cell phone from my back pocket and looked down at the screen to see another missed call from Tess. It'd been two weeks since I talked to Rob or anyone. I leaned back in my chair and closed my eyes. God, I missed her, but I had to stay away until I figured this shit out. There was no way I could have been around them while trying to avoid Rob. It was extreme, but I refused to be the cause of any more heartache for that man. Until I knew my life's direction, I had to stay away. Simple as that.

Hearing my cell ring again, I saw a California number.

"Hello?"

"Hello, Naomi. It's Kirt. How are you, Dove?"

Hearing my old friend's voice filled me with joy.

"Kirt! Omg, how are you? I've missed you so much!"

"I'm good, Dove, I'm good. I'm still alive and kicking, giving these nurses hell," he said with a hearty laugh that turned into a rough cough.

"Are you alright?" I asked, not liking the sound of that cough.

I heard him sip something. "Yes, I'm fine. That pneumonia is a tricky bugger; as soon as I think I'm on the mend, *WHAM* it comes and knocks me back on my ass again." He chuckled weakly, cut short by another round of coughing.

"I'm sorry, Kirt."

"Oh, hush now, old Kirt will be just fine. How is Texas treating you? Are you still painting?"

"It's been good. I hit a rough patch and had to call Dr. Tracy, but it's getting better. And, of course, I'm still painting. I have a little protege of my own now." I shared with pride, thinking of Nate Jr.

"Oh, that's good, Naomi, that's real good. How old is your protege?"

"He's nine."

"Wonderful age! Start him out early. Please send me some of his work; I'd love to see it. When I last spoke to Dr. Tracy, she mentioned talking to you. Of course, nothing specific, just that you're still our strong Naomi."

I couldn't help but smile at that. "Is everything okay with you?"

"I hit a rough patch myself. You'd think once you reach a certain age, you'd have this thing called life figured out, and it's finally smooth sailing. Well, I'm sixty-eight and can tell you, that is a load of crap. I was doing pretty good until pneumonia knocked me on my ass. With all of the highs and lows that came with it, I figured I should call Dr. Tracy to check in."

"I'm happy to hear that. Hey, I have an idea! Maybe we could start a weekly check-in like we used to. I know that helped me a lot. I feel like I owe you and Dr. Tracy so much."

"Oh, stop; you don't owe me a thing. I remember walking into that rec room and seeing you withdrawn into yourself.

When I walked over and asked your name, and you turned those beautiful brown orbs up to me, I knew you were a fighter. I just had to get you to see it for yourself. Once you started to paint with me, you gave my dark life purpose again. You were the only one in the hospital that didn't know who I was. Everyone knew me as the world-famous Kirkland Vaughn, who had tried to off himself in a room full of people. When I was first committed, I didn't see the light anymore; I didn't want to paint. One dreary day, an angel was sent to me out of the blue. You didn't see the famous painter; you made me remember who I was. I hadn't felt that in a long time. Slowly, the joy of painting returned to me. I promised myself I would never lose it again. It wouldn't come second to money, fame, or prestige anymore. And I have you to thank for that, Dove."

"I'm so happy to hear that! You've helped me so much; I'm glad to know I also gave you something."

"And don't ever forget it. I have to go; the doctor just walked in to check on me. I will talk to you soon."

"Yes, you will. Call me if you need me."

"Will do, Dove."

CHAPTER TWENTY-FIVE

Rob

"So you're telling me all this went down, and I wasn't there?" Tess asked while we sat at her kitchen table.

"Yep."

"None of that dysfunctional shit ever happens to me. All my friends complain about hating their mother-in-law or beefing with girlfriends. My friend Tasha had to cut her husband's baby mama. Then there's me. I got a mother-in-love I adore. My brother-in-love doesn't keep girls around long enough for me to get into it with, and I will cut somebody about my ex-husband's current wife. I swear it must be me. Something has to be wrong with me. You should have called me Rob to tag me in or something. I blame you. But I am happy to hear you put them in their places. Even though I know he's not, Nathan should be ashamed of himself, with his sorry ass."

We were quiet for a minute before I blurted, "Tess."

"Nope, I don't want to hear it, Rob, I gave you my two cents, and that was to wait. I knew you both weren't ready."

"I love her, Tess. I tried to keep it platonic, but the more I got to know her, I was a goner. I swore after that shit with Brie; I was done. I planned to have a cutie in every city like Tee. There was no chance of me ever settling down. But look at me; I'm here again; the funny thing is, I'm not mad about it. And what type of parents does she have?" I asked, thoroughly disgusted. "They basically told me she was a mental case and that I should run for the hills. The only thing they succeeded in doing was making me fight harder. I mean, could you imagine having parents like that? As crazy as you are, our parents have always been your biggest supporters. No offense, sis." I looked up into my big sister's sympathetic eyes right before she pulled me in for a hug.

"I know, Rob; I'm crazy about her too. I mean, where does something like this happen? My ex-husband's soon-to-be ex-wife is quickly becoming one of my favorite people. So I understand more than anyone, but you have to give her space."

I started shaking my head.

"I don't want her to feel alone like she has to figure all this out by herself. She's got us. She's got me."

"I miss her too, sweetie. But we're going to have to respect her wishes and stay away. I know it sucks. Let's hope she figures things out soon."

CHAPTER TWENTY-SIX

Naomi

"I'm happy to report Olivia is coming along nicely. After checking her recent X-ray, the bone is healing as I had hoped. Good job, Mom," Dr. Milum said before leaving the room.

"Did you hear that, Livy? You're almost good as a new baby girl!" I leaned over to pepper her pretty face with kisses, making her giggle.

"Yay! Can I finally spend the night with Nate Jr. and Nya's mommy?" she asked with hopeful eyes.

"Soon, baby, I promise, okay?"

"Okay, mama."

"Hey, do you want ice cream from the Underground Creamery?" I asked, hoping to soften the rejection.

"Yes! Maybe we will see Nate and Nya there with Uncle Rob. Come on, Mommy!" she sang with all excitement restored.

I miss those kids terribly, but please don't let us run into them with their uncle Rob today. I prayed as we walked to the elevator.

~

There was a knock on the door; I glanced at the time to see it was 7:13 p.m.

"Livy, your daddy's here; get your bag, baby girl," I yelled down the hall while walking over to answer the door. "Hello, Nathan; how are you?" I asked with a bored expression.

"Damn, Naomi, is that any way to treat your husband?"

I remained silent with a blank stare. I glanced over my shoulder, wondering what could be taking her so long. *She may need a little help.*

"You are probably still upset with me for calling your parents. Come on, Naomi, try to look at things from my perspective. I was a concerned husband and father. You were sleeping with the enemy with Tess and *her* family over there. I couldn't get you to listen to reason; I was desperate, Naomi. I was hoping your parents could open your eyes. I can see now that it was a huge mistake. I shouldn't have gotten them involved. But if you had only—"

"Livy, come on, girlie, your father is waiting!" I yelled over my shoulder, purposely cutting him off.

"Damn, it's like that, Nay?" he asked, shocked.

Our daughter made it to us with her overnight bag and favorite stuffed animal.

I glanced back at him. "Yep, it's like that." I turned to our daughter, bending down to adjust her clothes and give her a big hug and kiss. "Have a good time, okay."

"Okay, mama, I don't want you to be alone. Are you going to call Aunt Tess?"

"Aunt Tess! Oh my god," Nathan mumbled under his breath.

"I'm not sure, baby, I have to work, and I also want to get some painting done, so don't worry about Mommy; I have lots to do until you come home, Okay?"

"Okay, mama, I love you." As she walked past me, she said, "Hi, Daddy, I'm ready."

"Okay, let's go."

He turned to say something right after he grabbed her hand, but I closed the door. I was not ready to forgive him for what he did. I didn't know if I ever would be.

CHAPTER TWENTY-SEVEN

Naomi

Saturday afternoon, while at the gallery, I received a call from a Texas number I didn't recognize.

"Hello, this is Naomi?"

"Teddy, I got her ass, yeah Ladybug, it's me. Your ass thought you would get away from us that easily; you thought wrong, sis." Terrell laughed into the phone.

Hearing his voice made me want to laugh and cry at the same time.

"You are so crazy, Tee; what do you want? I'm working."

"Give me the phone." I made out Teddy's deep voice in the background, making me feel like a little girl about to get in trouble.

"Hello Naomi, it's Teddy."

"Hey Teddy, how are you?" I asked, trying to keep my emotions in check.

"Listen, I'm worried about you and want to see you. Terrell and I will stop by the gallery to take you to lunch in a half hour. Does that work?"

"Teddy, I don't know—"

"Listen, Ladybug. It will only be Tee and me. I need to see with my own eyes that you're okay."

It was the concern in his voice that made me cave. The only reply I could give was, "Okay, I will be ready."

"So Tess and Teddy met through you and Rob?" I asked Terrell, biting into my burger.

"Yep, I met Rob in junior high; we clicked from the start. Man, we caused all kinds of trouble once we linked up," he said, laughing.

"Wow, y'all have been friends for that long, huh?"

"Yep, that's my dog for life," he said with pride.

"I remember this one time when we were like fifteen; we got tattoos from a tattoo artist we convinced we were eighteen. We got in so much trouble my mama was even talking about sending me off to military school. You remember that, Teddy?"

"Yeah, remember that. How can I not? That was the day I met my angel."

"Angel? That woman was a damn demon! I will never forget that day. Man, Tess can scare the shit outta somebody with that mouth alone. Even though I was bigger than her at fifteen, I kept my ass at the top of those steps, out of her reach," Terrell said, chuckling, before imitating Tess.

"'No bitch you got it all wrong; I am my brother's keeper, not you. Making my baby brother get that big ass tattoo across his back. So come down here and get this ass whooping waiting for you,' she screamed from the bottom of the stairs, shooting daggers at me with her eyes." He had to hold his stomach from laughing as he retold the story.

"I heard all this commotion outside; the first thing I said was, what has Terrell done now? I remember stepping outside to see the woman of my dreams, hot as fish grease, at the bottom of our steps. Her nostrils flared, and her tiny hands fisted at her sides." Teddy chuckled. "After I calmed her down by promising to beat the shit out of Terrell, I asked if I could walk her home since the sun had gone down."

"Always the gentleman," I said to him, sipping my shake.

"Whatever, that woman was mean as hell," Terrell chimed in. "After smiling at Teddy, she turned those evil eyes back on me, 'I'm watching you; your ass has been put on notice.'"

I sputtered out some of my milkshake. His imitation of Tess was too good.

"Hey man, that's my baby you're talking about," Teddy warned playfully.

"I know *my sister*; I'm just saying Tess is not to be played with."

Teddy and Terrell laughed at the memory. "She kept calling Rob her baby brother, even though at fifteen he towered over her." Teddy continued to laugh. "I knew I had to defuse the situation because little mama was out for blood, my baby brother's blood."

"And the crazy part about the whole thing was it was Rob's idea for us to get the tattoos in the first place, but I was the bad guy. I'm still hurt about that. When I see her later, I will demand my overdue apology."

"What you're going to do is leave my wife alone."

"See, that's the problem right there, Ladybug," Terrell said, rapidly pointing at his brother while staring my way. "He's always fighting her battles."

"And I will continue to do so until the day I take my last breath."

"Just whooped," Terrell said, shaking his head in mock disgust. "It's sad to witness."

"Well, I think it's beautiful," I said with a smile. "And knowing Tess the way I do, I know she wouldn't hesitate to go up against the devil himself to protect her man. We can all agree that woman may be small, but she's mighty; test her if you want to."

"Agreed," Teddy said with a huge grin.

"Agreed," Terrell grumbled.

"How did you and Tess end up together?" I was curious to know where Nathan came from if they were teenage sweethearts.

"We dated for a while when we were younger but grew apart. We both had some growing to do. When I was twenty-one, I enlisted in the military and focused on my military career. Tess met and married Nathan. And we both were living our lives. When I retired from the military, I found out Tess was going through a divorce. I knew it was our time, so I went and got my woman. I wasn't going to let another man swoop my baby up. Not this time. We haven't looked back ever since. Nathan has been a fool if you ask me. He's lost two good women. I doubt if he will be so lucky a third time. I don't know what you have going on in that pretty little bald head of yours; know, we're family. I know you are going through some things, but I do not doubt that you and Rob will figure it out. And even If y'all decide friendship is best, we're still here. Now that's all I will say on that." He winked.

"That's right, sis. It may be awkward as hell during family game night, but it's all good. We are locked in for life. I now see you as my sister, like Tess, how I see Teddy as my brother, like my blood brother Rob."

"Wait, what? I *am* your blood brother, fool; what are you talking about?" Teddy asked, looking at his demented younger brother.

"Are you, though?" Terrell countered with a straight face.

I couldn't help laughing as they went back and forth, further lifting my spirits.

CHAPTER TWENTY-EIGHT

Naomi

"Please take some time to look over the commission split to see if it works for you. I have a couple of collectors who would love this piece. I will be giving them a call," I said as I marveled at the beautiful painting in front of me. "Your work is reminiscent of Basquiat's neo-Expressionist style. With the bold reds and oranges, paired with the street art vibes through here. Did he inspire you?" I asked the young artist.

"Yes, I love his work!" she exclaimed.

"You and me both." I grinned at her. "And right here, this dramatic deep purple-and-lime-green color-blocking technique you've used reminds me of a street artist I had the chance to meet when I visited São Paulo, Brazil. I love this!" I beamed at the bashful artist standing in front of me. "You are so talented, Muddy. May I ask, how did you get such a unique name?" I scanned the exquisite painting one last time before looking her way. She was gorgeous with her toasted-almond skin, steel-gray eyes, and blonde dreadlocks. Her facial jewelry added to her allure. I didn't get a Muddy, but I loved the uniqueness of the name.

"I got it from my grandfather. I loved drawing in the mud with a stick when I was little. He would always yell, 'Muddy! Where's Muddy? That girl has tracked mud all through the house again.' The name stuck," she said with a mischievous grin.

"So you're a self-taught artist?"

"Yep," she said with a proud smile."

"Wow, impressive. You should be very proud."

I carefully laid the painting on the table. "I wish I had that gift. I was fortunate to work with Kirkland Vaughn."

"Wait, *the* Kirkland Vaughn?"

"The one and only," I told her with a laugh. How people reacted when I mentioned my mentor and dear friend always tickled me. Kirkland Vaughn's work was well known around the world. He was rich and famous, but you would never know it by the way he acted or dressed. Who would have ever thought we would meet and become close friends in a mental hospital? That was a very dark time for me, but something beautiful emerged. Our close bond baffled a few folks: a young black woman and a jolly older white man with a thinning ponytail. We were a sight. He was so patient with me. I used to paint here and there when I was young, but it became my therapy in the hospital. Painting quieted my mind; it soothed something inside of me. He called me his prized pupil. I didn't know how many artists he mentored, but the compliment meant the world to me. He was one of the few people I could be candid with, so I cherished his friendship with all my heart.

"Okay, if you're okay with the conditions of B. Waters Art Gallery, we would love to showcase your art."

"Really! Thank you, Mrs. Wells."

"I should be thanking you; judging by this painting, I know you're going far, so stay focused and don't give up."

"I promise I won't."

After seeing Muddy out, I carefully picked up the painting and carried it to the back. "Damn, that woman has talent," I murmured, studying the picture when I heard someone come through the door. "I will be right with you," I called out, placing a protective blanket over the painting as I hurried back out front. "I apologize for the wait; how can I ..." I trailed off when I looked up. "Rob! Um, how are you?" I asked, shocked, not knowing what else to say.

"Well, I'm looking for a piece of art to hang in my office at work," he said with a sneaky smile.

Damn, he looked good.

"Yeah? What did you have in mind? Is there a color scheme you're going for? A style?" I tried to stay professional, but it was hard. My *dream Rob*, whom I made love to every night, didn't do the real version justice; the man was fine.

"Well, I've been sad and missing my lady like crazy. I was thinking of a painting that would invoke hope whenever I looked at it. You know, to help me remain hopeful that she will return to me soon."

A smile tugged at my lips as I listened to him tell me he missed me.

I took him around to show him the different paintings and explained their origin. I felt his eyes on me the whole time.

After the mini-tour, I walked him toward the exit. "Well, I feel thoroughly informed. Is there any chance you could swing by my office to help me out? I could use an artistic eye on this. I could pay you for your time. I promise it's all business."

I studied him for a while, taking in his innocent expression. *Innocent, my ass.*

"Ah, sure, let me review my schedule and get back to you. Does that work?"

"I will make it work," he said with a wink and slipped out the door.

That man, that man, that man. I got back to work with a huge grin on my face.

CHAPTER TWENTY-NINE

Naomi

"What is that man's problem?" Nathan had called five times in the past half an hour. For the past few weeks, he'd been relentless, showing up at my apartment unannounced, trying to take me out to dinner, and even popping up at the gallery to bring me lunch. I appreciated the gesture, but there was no point. He started fishing for information once he noticed I had stopped visiting Tess and Teddy's house.

He shocked the hell out of me when he finally asked, "What happened?" When I didn't offer any information, he said, "It was for the best. It was a strange and unhealthy friendship for everyone involved; maybe now you could focus on repairing your family."

I swear, the man was unbelievable.

I finally listened to his voicemail to ensure everything was alright.

"Naomi, I don't know why you're avoiding me like this, but I think it's time for us to talk. Please allow me to tell you what happened the night of the fundraiser. Maybe it will make you a bit more forgiving after hearing about my dilemma. Please call me back."

Hmm, that was my first time hearing this. I wanted to know if there was more to the story.

Alright, Nathan, I will give you a chance to explain. I can't deny I would like to know why he would do something so stupid.

~

Later that evening

"So, you didn't want to come across as ungrateful in your boss's eyes. Is that what you're saying to me right now?" I asked, leaning over my kitchen counter and staring at Nathan in disbelief.

"Naomi, don't say it like that. Don't you see the dilemma I was faced with? If I had turned down the 'gift,' I could have lost the account. And you know Albert has been one of my biggest clients to date. Do you get it now?"

I could tell he was relieved by the look in his eyes as if I was finally understanding. I had to see; it was all a misunderstanding and wasn't his fault.

"Let me get this straight once more, your boss sent over some celebratory pussy for a job well done, and you couldn't turn it down because you were afraid of coming across as ungrateful, but you were willing to risk your whole marriage. Is that what you're saying?" I asked slowly, making sure I had it correct.

"Naomi, I swear to god, you're the woman of my dreams. I promise I never wanted another woman; I just felt cornered."

"What were you supposed to do in such a difficult situation?" I offered.

The dense man answered me, not picking up the sarcasm.

"Exactly!" he said, throwing his hands up with relief in his voice.

"Wow, Nathan, you were between a rock and a hard place, weren't you? I mean, on one hand, you have your wife and your family, but on the other hand, you have your job. *Your job*, Nathan," I whispered for emphasis. "What would you like for me to say? That I understand? That I forgive you for having sex in our bed? In our home? That I believe you would never do it again. I could tell you all those things, but they will not change the fact; I will not take you back."

"It wasn't my fault—"

"Nathan, stop," I said, starting to get tired. "All of this was for nothing. The damage has been done. Let's try to move on and figure out our next step, okay?"

Dead air settled between us as we stared at one another before he turned and left.

I was not trying to cause him pain, but it was time for him to understand.

It's over.

CHAPTER THIRTY

Naomi

"Hi, Sandy. Do I have any packages?" I asked the office manager as I made my way over to the mailboxes.

"I don't believe so, but let me check," she said, getting to her feet.

"Thanks, Sandy," I mumbled absently, looking at a letter from the finance company for my car.

I opened the document and scanned it. *What the hell, a late payment notice?* "What is this about?" I mumbled as I grabbed my cell from my back pocket. I dialed the number and waited for it to start ringing.

"No sugar, no packages for you today," Sandy informed as she returned to her desk.

"Thanks again, Sandy," I said with a smile, hurrying out of the rental office.

After the third ring, he finally picked up.

"Yes, my dear wife, how may I be of assistance?"

"Nathan, I received a letter from the finance company. Is

there something wrong? Can you give me the date you paid the car payment so I can have them look into it?"

"That won't be necessary; I can tell you what happened; I didn't pay it?

"What? Why not?"

"Well, being that you're working and living on your own, I figured there was no need for me to continue to pay for something that doesn't benefit me."

"Benefit you, Nathan? I use that car to drive your daughter to and from school and doctors' appointments; of course, it benefits your ass. By way of your child."

"It was your choice not to come back home, Naomi. But if you're saying you won't be able to get our daughter to the appointments she needs, I will have to rearrange my schedule to ensure that doesn't happen. I need you to know this is a huge inconvenience for me, but as a parent, I must put my daughter's needs before mine. Just know there will be consequences for this." He disconnected the call.

That's it! I was tired of his games. It was time to put an end to this train wreck of a marriage.

CHAPTER THIRTY-ONE

Naomi

When I got to work the next morning, something was off. I moved about my day, trying my best to drown out the feelings of loneliness and missing Rob. Seeing him the other day only reaffirmed that I had to work things through to get back to seeing everybody. I heard my phone ringing from the other room and hurried to answer it.

"Hey Tee, how's it going?"

"Hey, Naomi."

Naomi? Hearing him say my name instantly put me on edge.

"What happened? Is everybody okay?"

"Teddy was in a motorcycle accident."

"Oh god, how bad is it? Is he okay?"

"I don't know yet. I'm on my way to the hospital now, but I'm about an hour out, and Rob is trying to get coverage for his patients so he can leave. I don't want Tess at the hospital by herself."

"I will leave now. What hospital is he at?"

"He's at St. Lukes."

"Okay, I'm heading there now, and please drive safe, Tee," I told him as I rushed to grab my keys to lock up and hurry out. "Please, god, please let Teddy be okay."

~

When I reached the hospital, I pulled into the parking garage and hurried inside.

I rushed up to the help desk in the emergency department and asked, "Can you please help me? My brother was in a motorcycle accident."

"What's his name?"

"Theodore King."

"I see him here; you said you're his sister?" she asked, eyeing me.

"Yes," I said without hesitation.

"He's in room 214; once I buzz you through those double doors, it's the last door on the left."

I was already in motion as I thanked her. Once standing in front of his door, I took a deep breath to prepare for what I was about to see. I pushed the door and stepped inside to see Tess sitting in the bed with a bandaged but alive Teddy.

"See, I told you she would make it here before everyone," Tess said to Teddy with a warm smile on her face.

"You scared the shit out of me, Teddy!" I said to him before I turned my heated eyes on Tess. "And I don't understand why you allow him to ride that death machine daily in the first place."

"Allow?" Teddy mumbled under his breath with a chuckle.

"Oh, home girl is mad mad," Tess said.

I released an angry huff, trying to calm my nerves. "You know what, I'm glad you both think this shit is funny; I got to get back to work."

Teddy nudged Tess in her side. "Go."

"I'm sorry, we're not trying to make light of the situation. As you can see, he's fine. He has some road rash from the asphalt and a few scratches, but other than that, he's fine. We're waiting for his discharge papers now, but I'm happy you're here; I've missed you so much." She reached for my hand.

We talked and caught up for the next twenty minutes until the nurse returned with Teddy's discharge paperwork. I told them I would meet them at their house, and I left out so Teddy could get changed.

As I walked out of the hospital, I finally breathed a sigh of relief. *That's my family back there.* This self-imposed isolation was over. As I continued toward my car, I saw a familiar figure stepping onto my path. Once our eyes locked, I took off running to him. He opened his arms wide ready to scoop me up. No questions or words were needed. Rob and I knew what this meant. I was ready.

I made it home after spending the rest of the afternoon over at Tess's. Rob had to return to the hospital but promised to be over as soon as his shift ended. I was still on cloud nine, walking up to my front door to see a large envelope taped to it. *What the hell is this?*

I grabbed it off before I unlocked the door and stepped inside. I walked over to place my stuff on the kitchen counter as I pulled the stack of papers from the envelope.

"What! This man can't be serious. He's petitioning for full custody of my baby. What the hell, Nathan?"

CHAPTER THIRTY-TWO

Naomi

"That man is the devil!" Tess yelled.

"He knows Naomi is an amazing mother; he's using this to try and control her. Oh, sick bastard. If he hadn't been unfaithful in the first place, she would still be with his sorry ass!" Her words dripped with razor blades.

"Stop, Tess, you know there's no judge in their right mind going to grant Nathan custody. I doubt if he sees this through. He's playing games. A fucked-up game, but a game no less," Teddy said, trying to appease his wife but unintentionally doing the opposite.

She turned to him with fire in her eyes. "Are you going to sit there and make excuses for that man Teddy? Whose side are you on, man?"

"Tess, stop; I know Teddy is on my side, and so do you," I told her as I walked back into the den.

"Humph, you could have fooled me," she said, crossing her arms.

Teddy got to his feet and went over and pulled her into

a hug.

"Baby, stop. I know you're mad at Nathan, and nobody is defending him. Naomi is a wonderful mother. Anybody with eyes can see that."

"Well, say that; I take this game he's playing seriously."

"So do I, baby. I want to protect Naomi and Livy too. I promise he won't get away with this. He will come up missing before I allow that to happen."

"Okay, now it's time for you to stop playing, Teddy." She nudged him while giving a side-eye.

The look on his face made me question if he was playing. He had to be, I decided.

"If he keeps playing, I will drop Nate Jr. and Nya off to him and make him keep all three since he wants full custody of some damn body."

Her laughter surprised me; I glanced over with a questioning stare to ensure she hadn't lost it.

"Girl, Nathan kept the kids for one week when Teddy and I took a trip to Hawaii for our anniversary. That man called me nonstop, checking when we were coming home. He complained about juggling getting them to school, their extracurricular activities, making sure they were fed, and still having to work. If you had talked to that man, you would have assumed he'd been a single father trying to make it on his own out here in these streets, trying to give his kids the life he never had. The man damn near grew up in Bel Air with his weak ass. I swear, I'm embarrassed to say I was once married to him."

"You and me both," I grumbled.

After I put Livy down for the night, I stood at her door and watched my precious girl. Did he think I would allow him to take my child away because he was mad he couldn't have things his way? I had hoped we could resolve this amicably; there was no reason to be enemies.

But since you want to play this game, Nathan, let's play.

CHAPTER THIRTY-THREE

Naomi

"Nathan, you need to call me. We need to talk about this. I have called and left countless messages with your secretary; stop playing games, and call me, please."

I'd been trying to talk to him since I received his papers, but now he wanted to play games. I was sick of his shit at this point. How did he think this was going to turn out?

On the third day, I'd had enough. If he wouldn't answer my calls and wanted to continue playing these childish games, I'd catch him one morning as he went to work. I was waiting inside my car when I spotted his Mercedes pull in.

"Here goes nothing," I murmured as I placed my coffee inside the cupholder and got out.

He was preoccupied with getting his stuff out of the car; he didn't notice me approaching.

"Really, Nathan? This is where we're at? I had to resort to ambushing you at work to talk to you?"

He froze, hearing my voice.

"My, my, my Naomi, I couldn't get so much as a text back from you a few weeks ago. Now you're blowing up my phone; how the tables have turned," he said smugly.

"What in the hell are you talking about? This is business, man. That's the only reason I've been trying to reach you."

"Oh, and it wasn't business when I wanted to talk to you? You and Livy are my *business*, and I was pleading with you to come home or talk to me about us."

"Nathan, that wasn't business, and you know it. Regarding the papers you sent me, that's *business*. What do you mean you want full custody? What sense does that even make?" I asked, following behind him as we walked toward the large brick building's entrance.

"Naomi, if you don't want to talk about couples therapy or us trying to save our marriage, there isn't anything to discuss. We will just let the court decide." He walked into the lobby.

I followed him inside, trying to talk some sense into the crazy man.

"Good morning, Cindy, can you be a doll and call security? My soon-to-be ex-wife is harassing me."

"Sure thing, Mr. Wells," she said before picking up the phone and speaking quietly into the receiver while looking at me.

"Are you sure you want to play this game?" I asked through gritted teeth.

He lifted two fingers into the air without turning around as he continued to the elevator.

"Uh, Mrs. Wells, I must ask you to leave."

"I'm going!" I yelled, pushing my way through the double doors.

Back inside my car, I started breathing deeply, trying to get my anger under control. It wasn't working, so I gripped the steering wheel and screamed. After that, I sat with my eyes closed. I refused to act irrationally and ended up doing something stupid. I was smarter than that. What I wouldn't do is allow him to get away with this. With a plan, I started my car and headed to family court.

CHAPTER THIRTY-FOUR

Family Court Mediation

Naomi

"It's unfortunate that Mr. Wells isn't interested in mediation," Ms. Fawn, the court-appointed mediator, said with a stern expression. "We could have worked together to develop a custody schedule that worked for everyone. It's also a shame marriage counseling wouldn't have worked, but I understand that catching one's spouse in infidelity would be a deal-breaker for anyone. I hate to see a beautiful family come to this." A haggard sigh left her thin lips.

"This is ridiculous and a waste of everyone's time," I told her, trying to keep my anger in check. "Nathan and I could have worked this out; he's choosing to be difficult. Despite how I may feel about him, he's a wonderful father, and I've always told him that."

"I must say, I was a little shocked when Mr. Wells requested full custody when his indiscretion led you all here." She tabbed through her notes. "I see here you're not requesting spousal support. May I ask why?" she said, a little baffled.

"I was hoping we could work something out for us as a family, but he's been difficult to talk to if it isn't about something he wants to hear."

"That's unfortunate for him. Can you think of anything that would make him act in the manner, Mrs. Wells?"

"Other than not wanting a divorce, no. It may be hard for him to accept right now, but it's for the best. Maybe we can be cordial enough to co-parent in peace in time."

"Okay, I will set a court date. I have a feeling things aren't going to work out the way Mr. Wells had hoped. Thank you for coming, Mrs. Wells." She released a reluctant sigh.

"Thank you, Mrs. Fawn."

I pushed out of the family court building, heavy with disappointment. I couldn't believe this man missed our scheduled custody mediation. Now we had to go before the judge. *That's okay; you've only made this easier for me, you idiot.* I fumed as I marched to my car.

CHAPTER THIRTY-FIVE

Later that week

Naomi

I was walking back to my car from dropping Livy off when I heard the faint sound of my phone ringing.

"Damn it, not again. I'm forever leaving that phone in the car." I hurried to unlock the door and reached inside to grab it.

"Hello, this is Naomi."

"Hi Nay, it's Dr. Tracy; how are things, love?"

"Um, great, Dr. Tracy; how are you?" I asked as I took a couple of deep breaths to steady my breathing.

With my eyebrows drawn together, I climbed into the driver's seat and closed the door. I leaned back and waited to hear the nature of her call.

"It's probably nothing, dear, but we received a call from someone inquiring about your time here."

"My time there?" I asked, taken aback.

"Yes, of course, I didn't share anything about you or the nature of your stay, but from what I could gather, they were trying to get information. I could tell he knew you were a patient here by the questions he asked. I got the feeling he didn't have any specifics and was fishing. I wasn't going to answer or confirm anything, but I did find it odd. I figured I'd better give you a call."

"Thank you, Dr. Tracy," I told her, trying to steady my galloping heart.

"No problem, dear, but I would like to ask, is everything alright out there, Naomi? Do you have any idea who that person may be? And why would they be interested in your medical background?" she asked with concern coating her words.

"Yeah, I'm afraid I have an idea, and I believe I know who tipped him off."

"Who would do such a thing? And more importantly, why?"

I couldn't believe how painful it was to say the words after they'd shown me time and time again how they felt.

After releasing a winded sigh, I told her.

"My parents. I guess they've decided to help Nathan."

It didn't take too long for Nathan to confirm my suspicions. I received an email that read,

"Oh, Naomi, I've received some pretty upsetting news about you that could potentially harm your chances of being alone with our daughter. As a concerned father, it is my job to protect my child. We need to talk. I will say that it's in your best interest to rethink your course of action before it's too late. Call me when you have time to discuss this matter further. Please know time is of the essence.

Your husband,

Nathan Wells Sr.

That bastard.

CHAPTER THIRTY-SIX

Naomi

Where was that red folder? I shuffled through all the papers on my desk with frustration. The gallery owners were super sweet, but everything was dated, which made my job that much harder. I was still extremely grateful to them though. I suggested different things to make the gallery run more efficiently, but they were not interested in changing a thing. So, I did my job to the best of my ability even though it killed me to overlook the potential this gallery could achieve. I looked to the far end of my desk, spotting a little red triangle.

"There you are!" I was too tired and mentally exhausted to do things right by standing and reaching over to grab the folder I needed; no, I had to do it the lazy way by leaning over and trying to finger-walk the pile of papers to me containing the folder I needed.

"Got it! … No, no, no," I chanted, watching helplessly as the papers tipped forward and began to free fall from my desk. With a loud huff, I spread my arms and placed my forehead on my desk.

After a few moments, I heard the phone ring.

"Damn, what now?" I snatched up the phone and brought it to my ear. "Hello?" I answered with a huff.

"Hey, Dove, did I catch you at a bad time?"

"Kirk! I apologize for being short; I've had a stressful day, that's all. Thank you for calling; it gives me a chance to take a break. How are you? Is everything okay?" I asked, remembering the last time we talked; he was battling pneumonia.

"Yep, good as new; I'm actually on my way to Brazil."

"What?! I wish I were going with you right now." I whined, meaning it with every fiber in my body.

"How did I know you were going to say that?" He chuckled, making me smile.

"Next time, Dove, I promise. We will plan a trip down there to check out the up-and-coming talent. My treat."

"Okay, you got a deal."

"My reason for calling is because an old friend out in Texas is retiring from the art scene, and her art gallery is up for grabs. I wanted to see if you were—"

"Yes! I'm interested; tell her yes!" I yelled, not giving him a chance to finish his question.

"I figured you would be." He laughed heartily at my excitement. "I told Sloane that I had the perfect someone in mind that would be interested. I wanted to check with you first to make sure it was okay to pass on your information to her. I also put in a good word for you. So if it's something you're interested in, I can almost assure you it's as good as yours. I don't know much about the details; I will leave it to you gals to work out."

"Thank you, Kirk. Thank you, thank you, thank you. This is the best news; I could use some good news right now. And yes, please feel free to pass on my information. Oh my god!" I screamed into the phone.

"Well, I'm happy I was able to brighten your day. I have to get ready to board my flight. You should be hearing from Sloane by next week sometime. I will call you as soon as I get back to catch up. Bye, Dove."

"Okay, bye Kirk," I told him as the call ended.

I couldn't have wished for better news right now. I'd dreamed of having a space to offer art classes for children and adults and couldn't believe it might finally be happening.

Not even Nathan could knock me off this high. I happily got my butt up from the chair to clean up the mess I had made.

CHAPTER THIRTY-SEVEN

Naomi

I was hit with deep sadness once I turned down the street to our house. The first time I saw it, I knew it was the one. It represented a fresh start and a new beginning with the man I loved. I'd fought hard to reach that point; I looked forward to finally living. And I did just that. We were happy. I had no regrets about moving to Texas or marrying Nathan. It was almost as if I was destined to be here, and I had him to thank for that. *I'm not the same Naomi I once was. I get that now.* If I had only one thing to share with someone going through something, it would be that life is filled with hills and valleys; you have to learn to embrace them both.

I pulled up in front of the house, armed to fight. Honestly, I didn't know if he was ready to hear what I was about to tell him. But ready or not, after today, he would realize he nor anyone else would ever use my past against me. I refused to hide or view my past as a weakness. It was time I showed him.

After exiting the car, I jogged up the front steps and rang the doorbell. *Here goes nothing.* I waited as I heard footsteps moving toward the door. After he opened it, seeing me standing there, his shocked expression turned smug.

"Hey Naomi, what brought you all this way?"

I had to suppress a smile because I could almost guarantee that the conversation we were about to have wouldn't go as he was thinking.

"We need to talk. Do you have a minute?" I asked, not wasting time.

"Sure, I don't know why you didn't just use your key, Naomi; you do not need to be childish about all this. Should I ask to take your coat, too, since you're choosing to act like a guest in your home?"

"Stop, Nate," I told him, holding my hands up. "I didn't come all this way to fight with you; let's go to the kitchen. I will make us some tea while we talk."

"Okay," he said, sighing in relief. "Now you're acting like yourself. Lead the way." He gestured for me to pass him.

In the kitchen, I grabbed the tea kettle off the stove to fill it with water as he sat at the kitchen table and waited for me to complete the task.

With my back to him, I dove right in.

"I know you know about my time in the psychiatric hospital, Nathan."

From his silence, I'd caught him off guard.

"I know you weren't given the specifics on why I was there, but I will share them with you. All I ask is that you let me get it all out; if you have any questions, can you do me a favor and hold off until after I'm finished?"

I glanced his way and waited for his acknowledgement. Once he gave me a short nod, I proceeded.

"I've suffered from clinical depression for most of my life but didn't know it. In the beginning, we didn't know what was wrong with me. My parents assumed I was just lazy or lacked motivation. It destroyed me whenever they would say this or compare me to my siblings. So I learned some pretty unhealthy methods to suppress my emotions and pushed forward. When I was twenty-three, I decided that I'd had enough. My depression was all-consuming, and I couldn't live with the pain anymore."

I stopped talking to make our tea; I placed his cup in front of him and took my seat. I took a sip of the chamomile tea allowing the warmth to soothe me before I continued.

"Did you ever wonder why I never took these off, Nathan?" I asked, showing my bracelets.

"Um." He stopped to clear his throat, leaning forward in his chair. "No, I didn't think they held much importance to you other than they were a favorite accessory."

I smiled while I removed the bracelets. "Six years is a mighty long time not to take a bracelet off, even if it is a favorite, don't you think?"

"Well, yeah, now that you mention it," he said while shifting in his chair once more.

"I'm not asking to make you uncomfortable; it was just a question." I took a deep breath and held out both arms to show him my wrists.

I couldn't watch as he stared at my failed attempt to claim my life. As we sat in silence, it felt so weird to have my bracelets off, knowing someone could *see*. The truth was, I was no longer ashamed of them. *I'm stronger because of them. I am a survivor.*

I jumped when his big hands cradled mine. He ran his thumbs back and forth across my scars. I released a heavy exhale before I continued.

"The day I was released from the hospital, with medication, therapists, and my will to live somewhat restored, I sadly noticed my world was no longer bright but dull as if I was looking at the world through dirty glasses. The trees were no longer vibrant green. The sky wasn't as blue as I remembered, but despite it all, I worked hard toward rebuilding while putting my mental health first this time. It didn't happen overnight, but over time as I continued living, doing the work and staying diligent. My world slowly started to brighten back up, little by little. And when it felt as bright as it could get, a man walked with the megawatt smile that took my breath away," I said, remembering the day we met in my father's office.

A small smile played on his lips, reminding me of Livy.

"I love you, Nathan, and I probably always will, but I learned long ago what's at stake when you don't put yourself first. Thinking back, maybe I should have shared this with you, and for that, I'm sorry. It hasn't always been easy to be open and share my past. The stigma around mental illness is awful. It prevented me from being honest. On top of that, my parents did not want anyone in their circle to catch wind that one of their children had a mental health condition. You know, it's bad for the image." I laughed without humor as I looked up into Nathan's sad face.

"It wasn't until recently that I truly accepted everything about who I am. I thought I had, but I now realize I was still hiding. I had become so damn good at it. Despite how things may end between us, Nathan, I want to thank you."

He didn't ask why, just tilted his head in question.

"I don't think I would have ever made it to Texas if I had never met you. This may sound cliche, but I feel like a butterfly ready to spread my wings and fly."

"I guess you have Tess to thank for that, huh," he said with a frown but with less heat.

"You could say that," I told him with a laugh. "If you don't mind, I want to share one last thing with you. It's something I wrote when I was in the hospital. I wrote this for my parents, hoping it would help them understand what living with mental illness was like. Sadly, they still chose to disregard it, but maybe it could help you be a little more kind if you ever encountered someone struggling or going through something."

I reclined in my chair before taking a deep breath and began to read the words I wrote on that dark day nine years ago. These were the words that have kept me fighting to stay alive as well as trying to help others in this fight.

"The Easy Way Out."

"I cringe whenever I hear someone say these words about someone who committed suicide. I don't believe people understand how strong you must be to take that final step off the ledge. To swallow that bottle of pills, to slit your wrists, or take that pill to stop your heart. I wish people making this statement could try putting themselves in that person's shoes."

I paused, taking a deep breath before I continued.

"Imagine going through life with so much despair. Day in and day out, it's forever present and always lurking. And to make matters worse, despair isn't something that remains quiet and waits to pounce when you're feeling down or a little blue. Oh no, despair is loud, obnoxious, and must always be the center of your attention. It's what you wake up to in the morning and what you go to sleep with at night. There are times you try giving despair a run for its money. When you foolishly believe you're prevailing against the constant mental attack on your psyche. But unfortunately, there's not only despair you have to contend with. There's anguish too. These two working together can bring you to your knees. And it's constant.

"So you have this battle going in your head each day, but life still goes on around you. You have to put on a brave face, interact with people, smile, and listen intently to what everyone is saying around you. You have to have the social cues ready to respond accordingly. You have to be engaging and strong; all the while, you have despair and anguish in your head, making you work much harder to hear what the outside world is saying to you.

"When you think of someone with a grim cancer prognosis, they look at months and months of debilitating chemo and radiation therapy. I commend them. They chose to fight! Fight this deadly disease with everything they've got. They are fighting to 'live.'

"Take someone with mental illness; they're also fighting. They're fighting to make it to the end and not leave behind brokenhearted parents, children, siblings, and friends. They are fighting to stay 'alive.' So they endure. They continue to hide the excruciating pain they're in. They continue to suffer in silence. They silently scream into their hands in their bathrooms and bedrooms to emerge with bright smiles ready to encourage, give hope, give guidance, and share why life is worth living.

"When you wake up in the morning, instead of feeling refreshed and rejuvenated, you instantly feel sorrow, exhaustion, and ..."

"Please stop, Naomi," Nathan said roughly.

I looked up into his light-brown eyes, shining with sadness.

"I love you too much to sit here and listen to how much you've suffered. Call me weak, but my heart can't handle it." He placed his hand over his chest.

"I know it's dark and depressing to hear. It's still hard for me to even believe I wrote that. I hadn't felt like that in many years; that was my lowest moment. But I chose to *live*, Nathan. It helps me to always check in with myself because mental illness is real! It's as real as any other illness, and people don't see it that way for some god-awful reason. My parents, included, can't accept that they have a smart, loving, ambitious daughter suffering from depression. It's sad, but it's their problem, not mine," I said with a swipe of my hand.

"Look, I'm only sharing this with you because I'm not ashamed of what I went through. I'm stronger because of it; hopefully, I can give someone else hope that desperately needs it. So if you were planning to use this against me in court, I wanted to make sure you had all the facts first."

I got to my feet and walked to set my teacup in the sink. I gathered my things and left out with nothing more to say.

As soon as I got inside my car, a deep and cleansing breath left my body, leaving me light and relieved. Smiling, I grabbed my key to put into the ignition and froze. My wrists were bare, and I hesitated. I automatically reached over to grab them from my purse and stalled. Briefly looking at the house, I bit on my lower lip, turned my head, and peered down the street. I gave my head a shake as my smile grew. I left those bracelets where they were, started my car, and drove home.

CHAPTER THIRTY-EIGHT

Resolution

Naomi

Tuesday morning, I sat in bed journaling, when I heard a knock at the door. I grabbed my cell to check the time. Not expecting anyone this early, I hurried to see who it was.

I opened the door and smiled.

"Good morning, Sharon. Do you have something for me?" I asked my friendly mail lady.

"I sure do, Naomi; I just need your autograph," she replied with a bright smile, reaching into her pouch to pull out a large yellow envelope.

After signing for it, I thanked her before closing the door with my knee and walking into the kitchen. I sat on one of the bar stools while pulling the contents out of the envelope. On the first page was a note from Nathan. It'd been a few days since Nathan and I talked. We were due in court next week; I figured I would see him then. Looking down, I began to read.

Naomi,

Let me start by saying thank you. Thank you for sharing your past with me. I also would like to apologize to you. That was a low blow even for me to invade your privacy in that manner; I am truly ashamed of what I've done. It's because of my actions that we're here. I didn't want to give up on us or let you go. I still don't, but I owe you that much to do the right thing by you. FYI, I've parted ways with Warren and Associates. I finally realized how out of pocket Albert was. Don't get me wrong; I take full accountability for my actions; I just now see how much of a fool I was; I played myself. You are an amazing woman, Naomi. I couldn't have asked for a more courageous mother for my daughter. Enclosed are the signed divorce papers and the signed approval of Ms. Fawn's joint custody arrangement. Please know I will always love you and truly wish you the best.

Nathan

I skimmed through the rest of the documents before dropping them into my lap. After I released a heavy sigh, sadness pricked my heart. I knew he would do the right thing. *Eventually.*

My cell phone rang from the other room. I set the papers on the counter and hurried into my bedroom. I glanced at the time and smiled.

"Good morning, Tess; how are you?"

"Why so damn formal, don't start no funny shit; I'm not playing with you, Naomi."

I giggled, before I told her, "He signed the papers?"

"Nathan?"

"Yep."

She was silent before she asked, "How are you? Do you need me to come over?"

Even though she knew more than anyone how badly I wanted this, she always checked in to see how I felt.

"I'm good, no scratch that, I'm great!" I told her with excitement.

"Uh good, you had me scared for a minute, girl, sounding all somber and shit. Now, with that out of the way, tell me about this art gallery—"

"Uh, Tess, I hate to cut you off, and I know you're trying to help a sista out, but I have to go see my man, like right now."

"Well, don't let me hold you. And make sure to tell your man to call his big sister later."

"Will do; I will talk to you later."

"Bye, girl."

I lingered for a moment as a tingle that started in my toes traveled all the way up my body at the thought of seeing Rob. I jumped to my feet and skipped into the bathroom to get ready.

Naomi B. Wells Gallery Grand Opening

"Everything turned out gorgeous, Naomi! You are so talented. I've always envied people gifted to create beauty like this," Tess said, marveling at one of my paintings. "And who gave you the idea to showcase local talent in your gallery? That was genius! I am so proud of you," Tess squealed, yanking me into a big hug. "Nate Jr. is so excited about the painting classes. Some of his friends' parents have already contacted me to inquire about the classes; I will send them your way, so get ready."

"Oh, I am. I'm hoping to get Livy and Nya in here as well. And I expect to see you and Teddy in attendance for my grown and sexy sip and paints."

"Girl, you know Teddy and I wouldn't miss that for the world."

"Naomi?"

I heard Robyn call out, pointing at my "Only Love" painting on display.

"Yes?" I asked, walking over.

"I hope you offer a payment plan of some sort on some of these paintings because, girl, I can envision this one here in my house, but this price is like three times one mortgage payment, and y'all already know Marcus would kill me." She exaggerated the last part, making me grin.

"Robyn, why must you always bring up Marcus? We are all well aware that you got a man now, damn girl, give it a rest. Please, shit," Mona called over to a beaming Robyn, who was too high on cloud nine to care what her friend was talking about.

"Yes, Robyn, we will offer payment plans for the originals. I understand it's a huge investment, but remember, that's a one-of-a-kind Naomi B. Wells right there; I can promise it's well worth the investment."

"Well, okay girl, this is me right here. I know for a fact Marcus would want to have it." She placed her marker on it.

"I can't deal with her ass right now; I really can't," Mona mumbled, throwing her hands up as she stormed off. We all laughed, watching her march to the other side of my gallery, away from a glowing Robyn.

"Was it something I said?" Robyn asked, knowing damn well she was getting on Mona's last nerve.

I felt a small tug at the hem of my skirt. I peered over my shoulder to see Rob. He looked so handsome he nearly took my breath away. I turned as he pulled me into his embrace.

"I'm so proud of you, baby," he said into my ear.

"Everything turned out amazing, just like I knew it would; now maybe you can help me with a small problem?

His warm breath on my neck caused me to shiver.

"I'm listening."

"Good; I'm going to need you to come back here with me into your office."

"Oh yeah," I asked breathlessly.

"Yeah, there's something I would like to show you in private." He grabbed my hand and pulled me toward my office.

As I followed him, I saw Tess grinning at me. She raised her wine glass to me before turning to talk to Teddy.

That was her way of letting me know she would hold everything down until I returned.

Because of that woman, I looked up at the sky occasionally to make sure I didn't see little pink pigs with wings flying by. If someone had asked me a year ago if my ex-husband's ex-wife and I could ever be friends, my response would have been quick, "When pigs fly." Now I couldn't see my life without her.

EPILOGUE

BBQ

Terrell

"Wait, stop; let me just talk to you for a minute. You just might like what I have to say. You will never know if you don't talk to me," I said, giving Zena, Naomi's younger sister, a sexy smile.

"I'm sorry, but I'm not as carefree as my sister. This whole situation is a little too strange for my taste," Zena huffed out. She turned on her heels and headed back inside.

I stared after her with my eyes glued to her behind. "I don't know, brother. She seems a bit much if you ask me. She's gorgeous as hell, but are you ready for that headache?" Teddy asked, walking beside me as we stared after a retreating Zena.

"Give me some time; I plan to make lil mama mine," I said with a frown as I watched Zena laugh at something her friend Elliott whispered into her ear.

I could feel Teddy staring at me, but he said nothing. Hell, I was shocked as shit; those words came from my mouth. I knew one thing for sure: Zena would be mine.

Naomi

"Naomi, I love you with all my heart, and I'm so happy we're talking again, but I have to be honest with you; it doesn't feel funny being in a relationship with your ex-husband's ex-wife's brother." Zena finished slowly to ensure she said it correctly, causing me to laugh.

"I did, in the beginning, because it's something you don't see every day, but now not at all. And what about you? I couldn't help noticing Terrell couldn't take his eyes off you."

"Girl, you have nothing to worry about there. There's way too many fish in the sea to do this, keep-it-in-the-family crap." Zena gestured with her fingers, then glanced over to me. "Uh, sorry, no offense."

"None taken, but I did want to ask you about Elliott. He seems nice, and he's fine as hell. Is there something going on there I should know about?"

Zena laughed. "Girl, no, El and I are just friends; we've been friends for years. When I told him I would be visiting my sister in Texas, he jumped at the chance to tag along."

"Oh, okay, but a word of advice about Terrell, he can be pretty smooth," I warned.

"Thanks, but it's not necessary. I can guarantee nothing will ever happen between us."

"Okay," I said with a smile.

Rob

"I bet you end up having twins again, sis."

"You can go straight to hell, Robert; the doctor assured us he only saw one baby." Tess's heated reply came as she sat on the arm of Teddy's chair as he lovingly rubbed her stomach.

In the distance, I heard the doorbell.

I got to my feet and headed inside. "Hey, Tess, were you expecting anyone else?"

She turned to look at everyone. "Um, no. Everyone I invited is here. It's probably one of Nate Jr.'s friends coming to play video games."

"Oh, okay, I will tell them he will be home later. I leaned over and kissed Naomi's gorgeous lips, tasting the rum and coke Terrell made her. I jogged inside to answer the door, thinking about my lady.

Yeah, baby, drink up; I need you nice and liquored up for the nasty things I have planned for you tonight.

I was still chuckling when I opened the door.

"What are you doing here, Brie?"

I never thought I would ever see this woman again, but here she was, in the flesh, holding a *little boy.*

I let out a low chuckle, and at the same time, my heart kicked.

We stood there, staring at each other as my mind put the pieces together.

"Let me guess; you never got the abortion like you told me and kept my baby?"

"Yes and no?" was her odd reply.

"What does that mean? I don't have time for your games, Brie, so spit it out," I told her, hearing my blood rushing in my ear.

"Is there someplace we can go talk?"

I remained silent, resting my hand on the top of the door.

"Alright, I guess we'll do this now. To answer your question, yes, I kept the baby, but no, he's not your son Rob."

That knocked the wind out of me; I took a chance to look at the little boy in her arms. He looked to be the age our child would have been.

"What game are you playing, Brie? I can easily guess his age and do the math; why else would you be here?"

"Don't do this, Brie; he's finally happy."

I heard Terrell say from behind me. I saw him walking up with an expression I couldn't read.

"What about my happiness? I'm sorry, Terrell, he needs to know."

Guilt clouded his face as he stopped next to me.

My mind was trying hard to process what was going on. I turned back to Brie to see her expression mirrored Terrell's as my head volleyed back and forth, finally understanding.

My heart damn near seized up as I stared into my best friend's guilty eyes.

It all made sense now.

"It wasn't for me, was it?" I absently asked her.

I looked back to Terrell. "That pregnancy announcement in your car that day, it wasn't for me; it was for him."

Terrell lowered his head before telling me, "I'm … I'm sorry, Rob."

NOTE

Stay up to date on Daphne Kane's new releases and giveaways. Join her mailing list now!

https://mailchi.mp/0a2a6bd8d81a/untitled-page

AFTERWORD

Hello dear reader!

Thank you for taking a chance and reading The Sister Wife book one in the A Test of Love duet.

To find out what happens next and for the release date of book two in the duet My Brother's Keeper, join my mailing list now!

If you enjoyed the book, I would appreciate an honest review. Reviews help so much! Thank you!

Daphne Kane

ABOUT THE AUTHOR

Daphne Kane is an amazing mother and an emerging author from San Jose, California. She is an active and vibrant individual with a charming and enigmatic personality that helps her captivate and inspire everyone around her. Daphne is a vocational nurse and has a vested interest in giving back to the community.

Daphne always had a knack for writing, and the drive to share her stories and make people's lives better inspired her to become an author. As an author of contemporary fiction, BWWM, women's fiction, and American romance novels, Daphne aspires to bring her readers the perfect blend of heart, heat, and humor. She always hopes to write stories that make her readers laugh, maybe cry, but always happier than when they started reading.

When Daphne is not working, she loves to spend time with her three sons. She loves her solitude. Her home is her heaven. She keeps the creative juices flowing by keeping herself busy with making artwork, sewing, decorating, and dreaming up new stories.

Connect with Daphne online:
Daphnekanebooks.com

Goodreads:
goodreads.com/author/show/22451639.Daphne_Kane

facebook.com/Authordaphnekane
instagram.com/daphnekanebooks
tiktok.com/@daphnekaneauthor

www.ingramcontent.com/pod-product-compliance
Lightning Source LLC
Chambersburg PA
CBHW020109310726
48970CB00002B/545